The Goose Prince

Georgie lifted the window. The sash slid easily to the top. "Oh, hello there," whispered Georgie.

The Goose Prince was a little comical, seen close up. His long beak was like a big nose, and his two round eyes bulged a little away from his head. His webbed feet turned in like a pigeon's. He spoke, and it was like a flute talking.

"Would you like to fly around the pond?" said the Goose Prince.

"Oh, yes!" Georgie climbed out the window and stood on the roof of the porch, gripping the shingles with her bare feet, shivering a little in the night air. Then she turned quickly around, reached back through the window, and pulled Eddy's jacket from the back of the rocking chair.

Georgie climbed on the Goose Prince's back. He waited patiently while she tried lying forward and tucking her head into the space between the base of his throat and his left wing. Georgie locked her thin arms gently around his chest. Now her knees fitted perfectly behind his wings.

The Goose Prince curved his neck and looked back at her kindly. "Are you all right now?" he said.

"I'm fine," said Georgie.

"Well, then, hold on tight," said the Goose Prince. And then he took off.

THE HALL FAMILY CHRONICLES

◆

The
Fledgling

JANE LANGTON

The Hall Family
Chronicles

■ HarperTrophy®
An Imprint of HarperCollins*Publishers*

Harper Trophy® is a registered trademark
of HarperCollins Publishers Inc.

The Fledgling
Text copyright © 1980 by Jane Langton
Illustrations copyright © 1980 by Erik Blegvad
All rights reserved. No part of this book may be used or
reproduced in any manner whatsoever without written permission
except in the case of brief quotations embodied in critical articles
and reviews. Printed in the United States of America. For information
address HarperCollins Children's Books, a division of HarperCollins
Publishers, 10 East 53rd Street, New York, NY 10022.
Library of Congress Cataloging-in-Publication Data
Langton, Jane.
The fledgling.
Ill. by Erik Blegvad.
Summary: Georgie's fondest hope, to be able to fly, is fleetingly fulfilled
when she is befriended by a Canada goose.
ISBN 0-06-023678-7 — ISBN 0-06-023679-5 (lib. bdg.)
ISBN 0-06-440121-9 (pbk.)
[1. Canada goose—Fiction. 2. Flight—Fiction. 3. Fantasy.] I. Blegvad, Erik.
II. Title.
PZ7.L2717F   1980
79-2008
[Fic]

Typography by Larissa Lawrynenko
14 15 16 17 18 OPM 20
❖
First Harper Trophy edition, 1994
Visit us on the World Wide Web!
www.harperchildrens.com

For Chris

I think that no experience which I have today comes up to . . . the experiences of my boyhood. . . . Nature developed as I developed, and grew up with me. . . . In youth, before I lost any of my senses, I can remember that I was all alive. . . . This earth was the most glorious musical instrument, and I was audience to its strains. . . . The morning and the evening were sweet to me, and I led a life aloof from the society of men.

In Wildness is the preservation of the World.

—HENRY THOREAU

Contents

The
Fledgling

I

THE PRESENT

THE OLD GOOSE FOUND the present at Walden Pond. The flock had flown all day, and all the night before, and all the day before that, migrating from their summer breeding grounds at Hudson Bay. Tired and hungry, they dropped to the still evening surface of the pond, splashing down in great foaming sprays of water, squawking at the tops of their lungs, *a-WARK, a-WARK!* Then, drifting silently like a majestic fleet of ships, they moved in the direction of the southern shore.

All but the old goose. Turning away, he paddled by himself to a sheltered cove on the other side of the pond, heading for a place he remembered from years gone by, a place where acorns were scattered thickly on the ground.

And then he saw the present.

It was bobbing in the shallows, floating in the water, bumping the alder stems, nudged by empty beer cans, brushed by downy pinfeathers that had scudded across the pond.

It was a bright object, moving up and down in the small lapping waves, glowing by itself in the dusky air.

The old goose had never seen anything like it. Journeying south, year after year, gazing down at the landscape streaming away below him, he had sometimes seen the Atlantic Ocean alight with glowing sea creatures. But they were not like this.

Carefully the old goose picked the thing up in his beak and carried it ashore. Then, waddling slowly up the steep wooded slope, he found the place he remembered, where ten stone posts stood erect in a shadowy clearing.

The thing was a present.

Something solemn and compelling in the air of the quiet clearing seemed to speak to him, to tell him that. It was a present, and he must give it to someone.

The old goose shuffled with his webbed feet in the dry leaves beside one of the stone posts, making a hollow place like a nest. Dropping the present into it, he covered the glowing surface with another thick layer of leaves. Then he waddled slowly back to the water, turning the matter over in his mind.

He must give the present to someone. Not just anybody. Oh, no! It was too good for just anybody. He must give it to someone who would understand how precious it was. Someone who would take good care of it. But who? That was the question.

2

GEORGIE

*G*EORGIE WAS READING a book on the landing of the front-hall stairs. The window on the landing was open. She looked up to see the wind tossing the branches of the big tree outside.

If one leaf touches another leaf, thought Georgie, it doesn't make any noise at all. But when all the leaves touch each other, the tree whispers all over.

Then she saw the big birds in the sky. They were flying over the tree, making a loud noise, *a-WARK*, *a-WARK!*

Oh, swans! thought Georgie.

She jumped up and watched the swans fly in a ragged line over the house. They were not white like swans in a book. They were white and gray and black. They were flying so low over the tree Georgie could hear the sound of the air flowing through their feathers. It made a soft noise, *sssh, sssh, sssh.*

If only I could fly like that, thought Georgie. If only I could do it again.

Because she had done it. She had. She knew she had. She had waked up in the middle of the night. She had jumped down the stairs in two great floating bounds.

Unless it was only a dream.

Georgie turned around on the landing and looked at the twelve stairs falling steeply to the downstairs hall. Below her the bronze lady stood on the newel post, gazing as usual out the front door, holding her light fixture in one upraised hand. Her light was turned off. The hall was dark.

Only the white marble head of Henry Thoreau glimmered in the watery gloom. Henry was a statue in the curve of the stairs, a carved bust on a tall stand. Everything else in the front hall was nearly invisible in the murky shade of the downstairs, but through the oval glass of the door Georgie could see a piece of the front yard.

The sun was shining brilliantly on the green grass beyond the porch, and on scraps of long legs and big feet and shorts and skirts and blue jeans. Georgie's mother and Uncle Freddy were teaching a Saturday morning class in the front yard. Teachers and students were sitting in a circle on the grass. It was Uncle Freddy's school. Georgie's mother and Uncle Freddy had a school, right here in the house, and in the front yard and the backyard, and sometimes they even held classes way up in the branches of the apple tree. It was a college, really, with a funny name: The Concord College of Transcendental Knowledge.

This year they were studying a book by Henry Thoreau, who had lived in Concord, Massachusetts, down the road at Walden Pond, a long time ago.

Uncle Freddy liked to pretend Mr. Thoreau wasn't dead. He called him Henry, as if he were an old friend.

"Nice morning, Henry," he would say to the white marble bust in the hall, or "Henry, old man, listen to this," and then Henry would gaze wisely at the wall with his unblinking marble eyes as if he were listening with his stony ears and wondering and thinking it all over in his mind.

Georgie stood on the landing and listened. From the kitchen she could hear a murmur of voices and a clatter of dishes. Eddy and Eleanor were bumping around in the kitchen, having a snack.

She put her feet side by side on the top step. Then

she took something out of her pocket and looked at it. It was a milkweed pod from the meadow across the street. Downy seedlings were puffing out of the pod. Georgie pulled one free, tossed it over her head, and blew it high. The milkweed seedling twirled, then wafted sideways like a fluffy parasol. Georgie took a deep breath and blew it down the stairs. Lightly it drifted halfway down, and then it was caught by a little draft from the crack around the front door. Up it went again. At last it floated against Henry Thoreau's marble ear and clung there.

I can do that too. Georgie put the milkweed pod back in the pocket of her red overalls. *I know I can. Two big jumps. Just floating. I did it before. I think I did. I can do it again.*

Georgie clenched her fists. *I've got to. I've got to.*

In the kitchen Eddy and Eleanor heard the *thumpity-bump* and the thin squeal.

"Oh, no," said Eddy, jumping up, "it's Georgie! There she goes again!"

"Oh, poor Georgie!" Eleanor ran out into the hall after Eddy. "Georgie, not again!"

Georgie lay in a heap at the bottom of the stairs, a jumble of red overalls and skinny arms and legs. Whimpering, she looked up at the two big faces bending over her with the light from the front door fuzzing around their hair. "Honestly, Georgie," said Eleanor. Gently she picked up Georgie and sat down with her on the bottom step. Georgie pressed her face against Eleanor's sweater. "Now, promise me, Georgie dear," said Eleanor, "you won't ever do it again."

"You crazy little kid," said Eddy. "You know you can't fly downstairs. I told you that the last time. Next time you'll break your neck. Nobody can fly downstairs. Jump, maybe—sure, you can jump. But you can't fly."

Eddy and Eleanor were much older than Georgie. They were like a king and queen, towering and majestic and kind. It was true that they shouted at each other sometimes, and even punched back and forth, or shrieked and slapped, but they were always nice to Georgie. "Look," said Eddy, "I'll show you how to jump, Georgie. Just move over. Come on, get out of my way."

"Don't push," said Eleanor testily, but she hitched over on the bottom step and squeezed up against the newel post, while Eddy demonstrated exactly how far it was possible to jump down the stairs. His final mighty leap was a tremendous plunge from halfway to the second floor. Eddy thundered down with an enormous crash that shook the bust of Henry Thoreau. Then he staggered to his feet, breathing heavily. "Just try it a few at a time, you see, Georgie. Work your way up. But don't try it from the top. You couldn't ever jump from the top of the stairs. Well, maybe after years of practice, sure. But not now."

Eleanor was scornful. "Oh, Eddy, Georgie doesn't want to jump down the stairs. Look, Georgie, I'll show you something better than jumping. Something that feels like flying, it really does. Are you all right now?"

Carefully Eleanor set Georgie on her feet, and then she stood up too. "Watch this, Georgie." For a moment Eleanor stood erect, scowling at the thick dark air, and then she ran forward and made a mighty spring. In midair she whirled around, her orange pigtail flying, and then she came down hard at the other side of the dim, hollow hall, facing the other way. Breathing heavily, she grinned at Georgie, feeling pleased with herself. "There, you see, Georgie? Didn't that look like flying? It feels like flying, it really does." I should have gone on with those ballet lessons, thought Eleanor. I could be dancing before the whole world right now, instead of just my kid brother and my little stepcousin who may be going crazy. "When you flew downstairs, that wasn't real at all, Georgie. It was just a dream. I mean, come on now, Georgie, really."

Georgie stared at Eleanor and waited a minute. (Georgie often waited a minute before she said anything.) "Well, I guess so," she said. "Well, maybe." But she didn't really think it had been a dream. It had been so bright! It had felt so lovely! She had flown! Like the swans!

The jumping and dancing lessons were over. Georgie went out on the front porch. "I'm all right now," she said, shutting the door behind her. Then she opened it again and put her head back inside. "Thank you," said Georgie.

Eddy shook his head and grinned at Eleanor. "What a crazy little kid." Then he looked up quickly. There was a noise in the sky. "Listen, you hear that? It's geese, Canada geese!"

A-WARK, a-WARK! High over the town of Concord the great flock of sixty geese was banking and turning, flying back from Walden Pond to feed on the marsh grasses of the Great Meadows. Their wings pumped strongly. They made a waving pattern like an arrow in the balmy September sky. From wing to laboring wing they passed the creamy air, gabbling to each other in their hoarse strident talk. *Go DOWN! go DOWN! go WHERE? go THERE? where, WHERE? here, HERE? no, THERE! there, THERE! come DOWN! down, DOWN! right HERE? yes, HERE! down, DOWN! come DOWN! right DOWN!* Far below them lay the town of Concord, its rooftops barely visible under the puffy green and yellow trees, the streets running straight and black, the rivers looping in round curves, flashing back the image of the racing sun.

The largest bird of all flapped heavily at the end of the line. No longer was the old goose flying with his mate, guiding another young family of excited half-grown fledglings from the blue northern lake where the goslings had been born. His mate had died long ago. He was a lone bird, old but mighty in wingspread, an out-sider, traveling with a busy, clamoring flock of younger geese—mothers and fathers and children, sisters and brothers, cousins and uncles and aunts.

Now the old goose slowed the rhythmical beat of his wings and lowered his long black neck to stare down at the roofs of the houses running away below him. One house was different from the rest, odd and tall, with a tower at one side. Straining his bulging eyes, he saw a circle of men and women sitting in the front yard. Their heads were lowered. They were looking down.

A small red person was standing on the front porch, looking up.

For an instant the old goose wavered in his flight, staring down at the small red spot. But then the circle of people in the front yard looked up too. They became a ring of white faces, gazing back at him, jumping to their feet, pointing upward. The old goose summoned the powerful muscles that flexed and stretched his wings, and caught up with the rest of the flock as it began its long gliding descent—down, down to the sheet of blue water and the sedgy marsh grass of the Great Meadows.

And all along Walden Street and Main Street and Monument Square, all the way down Monument Street to the North Bridge, people ran to the windows and looked up and smiled, pleased by the racket and the sight of the strong pumping wings against the sky.

"It sounds like fall," they said to each other. "When the geese come back, you know it must be fall."

3

WANTING THINGS

FIFTEEN STUDENTS WENT back and forth to college classes in the big house at No. 40 Walden Street, but only five people lived there all the time:

1. Frederick Hall was the founder and president of The Concord College of Transcendental Knowledge. Concord College was the best place in Massachusetts—no, in all New England—no, no, more than that, it was the best place in the entire United States—oh, no, no, that's not enough, it was the best place in the whole wide world!—to learn about the wise men who had lived in Concord a hundred years ago, Henry

Thoreau and Ralph Waldo Emerson and all their poet-friends and fellow thinkers.

Uncle Freddy was also the guardian of his orphaned niece and nephew,

2. Eleanor Hall, 14, and

3. Edward Hall, 12.

4. Alexandra Dorian Hall was not only the wife of Frederick Hall, she was his colleague and fellow professor. Before marrying Uncle Freddy she had been a student in his school, a widow with a little girl. The little girl was

5. Georgie Dorian. Georgie was eight years old, but she looked much younger—six, or even five—she was so small and skinny.

Of course, if you counted the animals that lived at No. 40 Walden Street, the list could go on and on:

6. cat,

7. cat,

8. cat,

9. cat,

10. cat, and

11. cat.

And then there were the pieces of statuary standing

14

around the house. They were almost like members of the family:

12. The white marble bust standing in the front hall was Uncle Freddy's "Henry." In real life Henry Thoreau had lived in a small house at Walden Pond with all nature at his doorstep, and he had written a book about it, called *Walden, or, Life in the Woods.* Of all the books in the world, *Walden* was Uncle Freddy's favorite.

13. "Waldo" (for Ralph Waldo Emerson) was Henry's friend. He stood at one side of the fireplace in the parlor.

14. "Louisa" (for Louisa May Alcott) stood on the other side of the fireplace. (Eleanor had once tried to marry Louisa's bust to Henry's, but Uncle Freddy had plunged in on the tender scene and forbidden the union.)

15. Last of all was the bronze woman standing on the newel post of the staircase in the front hall, holding up her lamp like the Statue of Liberty.

There, that was it, the whole list of residents at No. 40 Walden Street. It was a long and confusing list. But under the high peaked roof and within the swollen porches of the house, the five human inhabitants felt like an ordinary family.

Ordinary? Uncle Freddy sometimes wondered if it was ordinary for Eddy and Eleanor to yell at each other so much, to be so often at each other's throats. Again and again he was shocked by the fury that shook the house. And then Aunt Alex would say, "It's just a phase. Don't worry, Fred dear. I'm sure they're just going through some sort of phase."

But now it was Aunt Alex's turn to worry. She was anxious about Georgie. Was something the matter with Georgie? Once again she had tried to fly down the front-hall stairs. It was the third time. It was a miracle that she had not yet been hurt. Aunt Alex sat at the table in the parlor, grading papers with Uncle Freddy, trying to focus her attention on Arthur Hathaway's first assignment of the college year. But all she could think about was her daughter Georgie.

On the other side of the table Uncle Freddy looked up at her and beamed. "My dear, you must read this paper of Millicent O'Toole's. I am truly pleased."

"You know, Fred dear," said Aunt Alex, staring through the gap in the parlor curtain at the stairway in the front hall, "she thinks she can fly. She really does."

"Millicent O'Toole?" Uncle Freddy was astounded.

"Oh, no, not Millicent O'Toole." Aunt Alex laughed. "Georgie."

"Oh, Georgie, yes, of course." Uncle Freddy put Millicent's paper down, and then he too looked through the gap in the parlor curtain. The pale bust of Henry Thoreau gazed back at him like the old and valued friend he was. "Poor Georgie," said Uncle Freddy. "She is too young to know the limits of human possibility. For Georgie, anything is possible! She lives entirely in the pure ideal. And, after all, why should we not have been born with wings?" Uncle Freddy crowed like a cock, *AR-AR-AROOOO!* Flapping his elbows, he thumped up and down in his chair like a giant bird. "It's too bad! What a terrible cosmic mistake!"

"But she wasn't born with wings," said Aunt Alex, looking at him steadily. "And I'm really so afraid she may hurt herself. She's so certain. She really *believes* she can fly. It's because she *wants* to so badly. *Wanting* has turned into *believing*."

"Wanting?" said Uncle Freddy. "But look at Eddy. Do you know what Eddy wants? All the rocket models in the sporting goods store. He told me that. He wants them all. He's going to buy them one at a time and bring them home and sit up in his room, hour after hour, week in, week out, gluing them all together. That's what Eddy wants. What, I ask you, is going to happen to the boy's homework? And as for Eleanor, merciful heavens, when it comes to wanting things, there's no end to the things that Eleanor wants."

"But that's different. That's the way most children want things. But Georgie—" Aunt Alex hunched up her shoulders with worry. "Don't you remember when she wanted to learn to read? It was a passion with her. You remember—it wasn't just picture books. She was lugging that giant dictionary around with her. She *had* to read, she just *had* to. And she was only four years old! Well, that's the way it is now. She wants to fly. And she'll go on wanting it and hungering for it and jumping off the top of the stairs until she breaks every bone in her body before she gives up. She doesn't give *up*. That's the trouble. And this time no one can help her. How can anyone teach the poor child to fly?"

Uncle Freddy looked dreamily at his wife. "But maybe she's right. Perhaps she really can learn to fly. After all, the child is hardly more than a wisp of thistledown. I sometimes wonder myself why the wind doesn't just pick her up and blow her away."

"She *is* awfully small and spindly for her age," muttered Aunt Alex. "You know the way she just picks at her meals. She eats like a bird."

"Well, perhaps the birds will teach her how to fly." Uncle Freddy exchanged a long, piercing glance through the parlor curtain with the bust of Henry Thoreau. "After all, my dear, you know what Henry said. The birds, he said, bore messages that were important to his life. *The sparrow cheeps to the great design of the universe!* That's what he said. The only reason we don't understand their language, he said, is because we are not one with nature. But Georgie is. Just look at Georgie!"

For once Aunt Alex wasn't interested in Henry Thoreau. "Eleanor thinks Georgie spends too much time by herself. She thinks Georgie should have playmates. Eleanor thinks—"

"Eleanor thinks!" Uncle Freddy jumped up and began striding back and forth on the worn parlor carpet. "Eleanor thinks too much. Eleanor doesn't understand. Georgie has a great many friends already. The birds, I tell you. The squirrels. The flowers and the trees. She is a child of nature, like Henry. Have you seen her little house in the bushes? It reminds me of Henry's, that famous little house that used to stand on the shore of Walden Pond. Like Henry, she is basking on the bosom of Mother Nature! That's Georgie. Let her alone!"

Aunt Alex's grave face lighted up with one of her rare smiles. "Oh, Fred dear, that's what I said. That's what I told Eleanor. I said she should let her alone." But then Aunt Alex's face fell. "I wish she would forget about flying. I just wish she would."

4

THE BUSH HOUSE

A TANGLE OF BUSHES grew around the place where the old summerhouse had stood. The summerhouse was gone, but there was still an empty place in the middle of the bushes. Long wiry stems of forsythia arched over it like a lattice roof.

It was Georgie's bush house. After school Georgie crawled into it, carrying her doll under one arm. She sat down cross-legged in a nest of leaves with the doll in her lap. Dappled sunlight fell on her face in flecks and splotches. It poured in round nickels and dimes on the sleeves of her jacket. The jacket was Eddy's. That is, it had once been Eddy's. With lordly generosity Eddy had handed it down to Georgie. The denim of the jacket was heavy like armor. Sitting in Eddy's jacket now, swallowed up in it, Georgie felt stiffened with some of Eddy's bold courage.

She listened. There were bird noises in the sky, light chips of sound far away, small sharp scissorings and snippings. They sounded high and thin, like the air. Another bird sang in the apple tree: *Pe-^{ter!} Pe-^{ter!} Pe-^{ter!} Pretty-Pretty-Pretty!* He flew from the apple tree, jostled one of the arching stems over Georgie's head, landed on her shoulder! and flew away.

Georgie sucked in her breath. She sat very still. Would the bird come back? But he was gone.

She turned her head. Beside her cheek a smooth brown ball was stuck to a twig. Georgie put her ear against it and listened. She knew the ball was crawling with tiny bugs. But she could hear nothing but the cawing of a crow high overhead. A distant hum of traffic was the sound of cars and trucks on Route 2. A throb in the sky was a plane.

Georgie looked down. A green inchworm was crawling up her knee. She watched the worm inch his way over her doll and start a long journey up the sleeve of her jacket. She sat very still while he crawled up her neck and cheek. The inchworm tickled. Georgie giggled, but she didn't budge.

Georgie's doll was called Dollabella. Uncle Freddy

had made Dollabella from an ear of Indian corn. He had scraped off the dried kernels and set them aside for the birds, and then, impulsively, he had pulled some of the husks back down around the empty ear. "Look, Georgie," he had said, "doesn't it look like a person? See, the corn husks are a cloak and the silk is her hair."

Georgie had clapped her hands and taken the ear of corn to her heart and named it Dollabella. She had wrapped Dollabella in oak leaves tied with a ribbon. "Now, isn't she pretty, Uncle Freddy?"

"Indeed she is. A little woman of character."

And it was true. The poor doll had no face, but she had a quiet, friendly personality all the same, altogether different from the flouncy chic of the rest of Georgie's dolls.

It was time to get to work. Georgie swept the floor of the bush house clean of last year's leaves, and spread fresh green ones flat for a tablecloth. Then she set the table with a collection of precious things from the pocket of Eddy's jacket.

Three yellow elm leaves, here and here and here.
They were the plates.

Blades of grass in a heap on one of the plates.
That was the salad.

Milky stones from the beach. Vanilla puddings.

Dried winged seeds from the maple tree.
Cookies and crackers.

Acorn caps and tiny twigs. Teacups and spoons.

A burr basket stuffed with small flower heads
from the wild asters that grew on the other side
of the road. The centerpiece.

Georgie picked up an acorn cap and stirred the air in
it with a twig. "Would you like some tea, Dollabella?"

"Thank you," squeaked Dollabella, "I don't mind if I
do."

Georgie tipped the cup against Dollabella's face at
the place where the mouth would have been if
Dollabella had had a mouth. Then she picked up her
own cup, threw her head back, drank her cup of air-tea
to the dregs, smacked her lips, and smiled at Dollabella.
"Isn't the tea delicious? How about a cookie,
Dollabella?"

There was a rustling in the bushes. It was Eleanor,
on hands and knees. "Oh, Georgie," she said, "what a
nice tea party. May I come too?"

Georgie smiled broadly in invitation, and Eleanor

crawled into the bush house and sat down beside her on the nest of leaves. Eleanor had just had a bath. Her hair was set. She was hot and clean, with wrinkled fingers. Damp pinkness steamed from Eleanor and filled Georgie's bush house. "Why don't you invite some of your friends over, Georgie?" said Eleanor. "You know, from school. They could bring their dolls too."

Georgie waited a minute. "Well, all right," she said. But she didn't know if she would or not.

Eleanor was satisfied. "Oh, look at that," she said, picking up one of the maple seeds. "Those funny things from the maple trees. Look, Georgie, you know what you can do with these?" Eleanor pulled apart the seed and fastened it to the bridge of her nose. The dry wing of the seed stuck straight up. "See? It's like a rhinoceros horn. Isn't that great?"

Georgie picked up another winged seed, pulled it apart, and fastened it to her nose. "It feels funny," she said, giggling at Eleanor.

"Oh, wow," said Eleanor, "here's something else. A grass flute. Wait till you hear this." She picked up a thick blade of grass from the plate of salad and stretched it carefully between her two thumbs. Then she blew on it. The grass made a soft hooting noise, like music.

"Oh!" said Georgie. She was enchanted. She tried it too.

Nothing happened.

"No, look, Georgie. You have to stretch it really tight."

Georgie tried again. This time a thin flutelike noise came from the grass. Georgie was thrilled.

The bushes thrashed. Georgie and Eleanor looked up, startled. A huge shaggy head was ramming through the leafy gateway to Georgie's bush house. It was Eddy's enormous friend, Oliver Winslow.

Eleanor was outraged. She fell forward on her hands and knees and shouted at Oliver. "Oh, no, you don't, Oliver Winslow. You get right out of here. Come on, get out right now."

"Well, well," boomed Oliver, grinning hugely, "what have we got here?"

Eleanor punched him in the shoulder. Then she leaned all her weight against him and shoved. "Go on, Oliver, you big dumb—just get out. This is private, strictly private."

But Oliver was colossal. He brushed Eleanor aside like a feather and bashed his way into the tea party. Lumbering on his tremendous knees, he crawled right over the tea table and sat down on Dollabella.

"Oh, no," said Georgie. She pounded Oliver with her skinny fists. "Oh, move over, oh, please, please."

Obligingly Oliver butted Eleanor out of his way and

moved over. "Where'th my dolly?" demanded Oliver. "I want thum tea for my dolly."

Eleanor's face was bright red. Her hair was beginning to spring away from her head in fluffy orange tangles. She pummeled Oliver. "Out, out! Come on, just get right out!"

"No, wait," said Oliver, laughing, fending her off with one arm. "I've got a song. Wait till you hear. It's a nice song for the dollies' tea party."

"Oh, shut up, Oliver, you just shut up!"

Shrinking into her corner of the bush house, Georgie put Dollabella behind her back while Oliver held Eleanor's flailing fists at arm's length and bellowed his song.

Great green gobs of greasy, grimy gopher guts,
Mutilated monkey meat,
Little birdies' dirty feet,
Chopped-up chunks of little wormies' dirty teeth,
All in a bowl of blood!
All in a bowl of blood!
All in a bowl of blood!
That's my mother's newest tasty recipe,
All in a bowl of blood!

"Oh, Oliver, *stop*. You're absolutely *repulsive*. That's just *disgusting*." Eleanor punched and shoved. Oliver began crawling heavily out the doorway on his knees, doubled over with laughter. In a wild scramble the two of them tumbled out of Georgie's house. The bushes snapped back.

Georgie stood up and peered over the arching branches and watched Oliver pound down the cement walk to the street, roaring *All in a bowl of blood!*

Eleanor was rushing the other way, hurrying up the porch steps, going indoors. Her face was flushed. She was grinning!

Georgie was amazed. She sank back down into her house and looked at the remains of her tea party.

The burr basket was gone, fastened to Oliver Winslow's pants. The leaf dishes were tumbled every which way. Georgie sighed and got to work, cleaning up. But she could find only one piece of vanilla pudding, a single acorn teacup, and a couple of maple seed crackers. Not a single blade of grass. Georgie picked up what was left of the tea party, stored it in the pocket of her jacket, and crawled out of her bush house with Dollabella.

There was plenty of grass outside the house. Where the bushes ended, the lawn began. It was patchy and weedy and in need of cutting. Georgie put down Dollabella and plucked a long blade of grass. Then she stood up, arranged the blade of grass carefully between her thumbs, and blew. The grass trembled and issued its fragile sound, like a little horn, *hoot, hoot.*

And then, to Georgie's delight, there was an answering noise in the sky. She looked up. She had heard that noise before. It was the swans! They had come back! They were flying over the house! Their necks were stretched forward, long and black, their beating wings were gray, the sunlight on their chins and tails was a blinding white. They were shouting, *a-WARK, a-WARK!* Georgie counted them, one, two, three, four, five, six, seven, eight . . . she lost count. There were too many, a long undulating flapping row, flying in the direction of Walden Pond.

The last swan was the biggest. He was looking down at Georgie. He was! He was looking right down! And now he was slowing the beat of his wings; he was turning, tipping, dropping. Georgie gazed up at him and threw up her hand. Oh, swan, come down!

But there was a sudden commotion in the house. Uncle Freddy burst out on the front porch, shouting, "Geese, geese!" He stood on the porch staring up at the sky. "Oh, noble birds, welcome! I bid you welcome!"

Georgie's swan seemed to balk. He flapped his wings uncertainly, circling, and then he began to lift again, squawking, flapping strongly until he was high in the sky once more, then higher and higher, until he seemed as high as the racing clouds. In an instant he had vanished from her sight over the tops of the trees next door.

But Uncle Freddy continued to rant, quoting Henry Thoreau at the top of his lungs. *"Great birds that carry the mail of the seasons, welcome! In your wildness is the preservation of the world!"* When he dropped his arms at last, Georgie looked up at him dolefully.

"He was coming down," said Georgie. "The swan was coming down right here in our yard."

"Not swans, Georgie dear. Those were geese. Canada geese. They're flying south, you see. Stopping over in Concord on their way south." Looking down from the porch at Georgie's pinched face, Uncle Freddy suddenly felt clumsy. Somehow or other he had blundered. Flushed with his own foolishness, he didn't know what to say.

A car went by in the street. Another car. A motorcycle. Then nothing more. Everybody else in the world might have disappeared forever. "Well, I'll go in now, Georgie dear," said Uncle Freddy awkwardly. "My goodness, all at once it looks like rain."

Uncle Freddy opened the screen door and went inside. Then Georgie said, "Oh!" and bent down to pick up something from the grass. It was a feather. A grayish-white feather, fluffy at one end, smooth and shining at the other. It had fallen from the swan.

5

GEORGIE TRIES AGAIN

At SUPPERTIME IT BEGAN to rain. The sky thickened with clouds like inkblots, and then raindrops began pelting down, drumming on the cement walk and the roof of the porch and the slanting wooden doors over the cellar stairs. There were rumblings of thunder. The dishes clicked and rattled on the shelves. Four cats meowed at the back door. Georgie opened the door, and the cats came streaking in, soaking wet.

Uncle Freddy was talking about the house next door. It had been sold, and the new owner had moved in. "I called on our new neighbor this afternoon," said Uncle Freddy.

"Who is it?" said Eleanor and Edward together,

looking up eagerly from their dessert.

"Madeline Prawn."

"Miss Prawn?" They were horrified. "Oh, no, not Miss Prawn!" There were groans of dismay.

"Miss Prawn," repeated Uncle Freddy dismally. "Miss Madeline Prawn."

Miss Prawn was not popular with anybody at No. 40 Walden Street. She was the personal secretary of Mr. Ralph Alonzo Preek, the president of the Thoreau Street Bank. Mr. Preek wasn't anybody's favorite fellow citizen either.

Uncle Freddy tried to make the best of things. "Miss Prawn was out in her front yard today, digging up the grass. I think she's making a flower bed. Maybe it will be nice to look out the window at Miss Prawn's flowers."

"Oh, no, ugh, ugh," said Eddy. "Not if we have to look at Miss Prawn at the same time. I hope she digs a hole all the way to China and falls through."

Eleanor cackled and scraped up the last of her applesauce. "Down the hole with Miss Prawn!"

Georgie's applesauce was untouched. She gripped her spoon tightly, then put it down, and looked at her mother. "What do the swans do in the rain?" she said.

"Swans?" said her mother.

"Geese," explained Uncle Freddy, smiling at Georgie. "She means geese. Canada geese."

"Oh, geese, of course," said Aunt Alex. "Why, they're fine in the rain, Georgie dear. They're water birds, after all. Don't forget that."

"They've got this oil on their feathers, Georgie," said Eddy. "Goose grease."

"No, no," said Uncle Freddy. "Goose grease is when you have roast goose, and the fat collects in the pan, and then . . ." Uncle Freddy stopped and looked at Georgie. "Or then again maybe you don't. You wouldn't have roast goose unless it was the hunting season. I mean, right now it would be against the law to shoot a goose."

He was making it worse and worse. Georgie put one spidery hand on his sleeve. "Do people shoot them? Do they really?"

"I'm afraid so," said Uncle Freddy sorrowfully. "But only during the hunting season. And the hunting season doesn't last long. But I agree with you, Georgie dear. Those noble birds! What a terrible thing!"

After supper the sky cleared. The air was fresh. The leaves were moist and dripping. A thin mist hung low between the trees. Faraway houses were dim. Trees loomed hugely in the fog.

Georgie came out on the porch after sunset, carrying Dollabella. The air was thick with dusk. It looked heavy and solid in layers of shadow. Thick enough to hold me up, thought Georgie, like the water in Walden Pond.

She put Dollabella down on the floor of the porch and felt in her pocket for the feather of the swan. No, no, it wasn't a swan. It was a goose. It was a goose's feather. Georgie stood on the top step of the porch stairs and tossed the feather over her head. The feather twirled airily and landed far away on the front walk. Then Georgie bent her knees and spread her arms to the side and jumped lightly off the porch. She came down beside the feather. She picked it up. Then she turned around and looked back at the porch. Had she lifted a little? It had felt nice.

Inside the house in the parlor Eleanor was making a dress. She was crouched over the sewing machine, driving her yellow cloth through it. The sewing machine felt like a motorcycle, and she was hunched over the handlebars, as the belt-driven wheel whirled and the motor buzzed and whined. Her foot pressed down on the button that lay beneath the table on the floor, then lifted and pressed down again. Start, *bzzzzzzzzzzzzzzzz*, stop, click the lever up, whip the cloth around, flick the lever down, start again, *bzzzzzzzzzzzzzzzz*. The yellow cloth was bright with orange splotches.

Eddy was doing his homework at the table. The homework was boring. It was only the second week of school, but he was tired of school already. In class he would slump down in his chair with his eyes half shut, trying to be invisible, but already his Social Studies teacher had learned to look sharply past everybody else and say, "Edward, what do *you* think?"

Eddy lifted his eyes from his homework and gazed dreamily out the window. Then he jerked up in his chair and stared. "Hey, Eleanor, did you see that?"

Eleanor didn't hear. Her dress was whizzing through the machine. The grinding of the motor pounded in her head. She didn't look up.

Eddy got out of his chair and parted the parlor curtain. The hall was dark. He put out his hand and felt the smooth round marble head of Henry Thoreau. Georgie was coming in the front door, noiselessly, like a moth in the gloom.

"Say, listen here, Georgie," said Eddy, "didn't I see you just now—"

"Oh, Eddy, look," said Georgie. She was holding something up for him to see. "I made Dollabella a new dress. See? It's ferns. It's all made of ferns."

"Oh," said Eddy, "Dollabella. Well, well. Good old Dollabella. Hurray for Dollabella."

Eddy dropped the curtain and went back to his homework. He must have been mistaken. He couldn't have seen what he thought he saw. That Georgie. She certainly was a nutty little kid.

34

6

THE EXPEDITION

NEXT MORNING BEFORE dawn the geese flapped up from the marshy water of the Great Meadows. In a frenzy of splashing and hoarse calling, they flew over the town and headed south in the direction of Walden Pond.

Uncle Freddy and Aunt Alex lifted their heads as the flock darted over the house, crying, *wake-UP, wake-UP!* Uncle Freddy smiled sleepily and murmured aloud, *"A clanking chain. A clanking chain drawn through the air."* (It was something Henry had said.) Aunt Alex smiled too, and then they both put their heads down and went back to sleep.

Eleanor half woke too at the sound of the geese.

Groaning, she turned over and fell asleep again.

Eddy was a sound sleeper. He never woke up at all.

Only Georgie came fully awake as the geese flew over the house. Jumping out of bed, she ran to the window. And then she saw him. She saw her swan. Her own special swan. He was bigger than the rest, like a king or a prince. A swan prince! The Swan Prince was flying at the end of the flock. They were winging low over the housetops, their long necks stretched forward. Only the Swan Prince was looking down. Could he see her at the window? She watched him fly away with the others. He was trailing a little behind them, looking back.

Georgie stared at the empty sky. Where were they going? She thought about it for a minute, and then she knew. They were flying toward Route 2. Maybe they were heading for Walden Pond. Walden Pond was just down the road. She could go there. She would! She would walk to Walden Pond! She would walk there and be back before school!

Georgie turned to the rocking chair where her clothes were folded in a neat pile. She felt keen and fresh and wide awake. She pulled off her pajamas and got dressed in a clean jersey and yesterday's red overalls. Then she stopped and looked at her shoes and socks. Eddy's green rubber boots were in the coat closet

36

downstairs. The boots would be better for an expedition. They would be too big, but she would wear lots of socks. Georgie pulled on three pairs of socks. Then she put her pajamas under her pillow and made her bed and laid Dollabella in the middle of the pillow. Padding softly downstairs in the silent house, she tiptoed into the kitchen to make herself a picnic breakfast. Carefully and quietly, pulling out the drawers slowly, setting things down on the counter softly, Georgie made a peanut-butter-and-grape-jelly sandwich, wrapped it in a paper napkin, and stuffed it into the bib pocket of her overalls. She put a ripe banana in one of the side pockets. Then she put away the peanut-butter jar and the jelly and left the sticky knife in the sink. One of the cats was meowing and rubbing against her leg. Georgie gave it a saucer of milk. Then she went to the coat closet under the front-hall stairs and opened the door. She pulled the string hanging down from the bulb. Light flooded the thick coats and the tumble of boots. The closet smelled of warm rubber and moth flakes and woolen cloth. Georgie put on Eddy's jacket. Then she found his big green boots. She sat down on the hall carpet and pulled them on. They were much too big, but the three layers of socks filled up some of the extra room, and they felt fine. Georgie stood up and walked to the front door, lifting up the big boots and putting them down as softly as she could. At the door she stopped. She was thinking of her mother. Her mother would be coming into her bedroom later on to wake her up for school.

Georgie crept back into the kitchen. Eddy's notebook was lying on the kitchen table. Georgie took a piece of paper out of it and wrote a note:

HAVE GONE TO FIND SWANS.

A moment later, closing the front door gently, Georgie remembered that they weren't swans, they were geese. It didn't matter. She didn't go back to fix it. She walked to the top of the porch steps and paused. Should she jump? No, her boots were too heavy for jumping. Softly Georgie walked down the three steps to the cement walk in front of the house and looked at the enormous star hanging low over the pink place where the sun was waiting to come up.

Georgie had figured it out. She knew what stars were. They were pinholes in the sky, letting the white fire shine through. This star's pinhole must be very large, the star was so bright.

It was a windy morning. Across the Mill Brook meadow Georgie could see the old elm trees on Lexington Road lifting the trailing ends of their branches and letting them go again. A brisk breeze was whipping down Walden Street.

She would take the shortcut. Georgie clumped past her bush house, past the laundry line, and started to walk through the yard of the house next door. Then she stopped short. She had forgotten that the house was no longer empty. It had been sold, and the new owner had moved in. The new owner was right there in her front yard, down on her hands and knees before dawn with a trowel in her hand, looking up sharply at Georgie.

It was Miss Prawn, Miss Madeline Prawn.

7

MADELINE PRAWN

*T*WO THINGS WERE more important than anything else in the world to Madeline Prawn:

1. Hard work
2. The finer things of life

Hard work was something Miss Prawn knew how to do. There was boundless energy in her thin, nervous frame. At the bank she worked very hard indeed, bustling from Mr. Preek's desk to her own, typing up letters and mortgage agreements and loans, running her bony finger down columns of figures, popping documents in and out of her tidy, well-organized files.

At home she worked even harder. In exactly two days Miss Prawn had rearranged all the furniture in her new house until it looked just right. She had pushed and pulled at chairs and sofas, shoving them here and there with all the strength in her stringy arms and wiry legs. She had banged up nails for pictures. She had dusted the pantry shelves and unpacked all her dishes and stacked them on the shelves.

So much for the hard-working part of Miss Prawn's daily life. The finer things were more spiritual. They were bits of sentimental poetry and albums of dark old pictures and folders of art songs spread out on the piano. They were

THE REVERIES OF MADELINE PRAWN

—a notebook with a padded silk cover. The pages of the notebook had once been blank, but now they were covered with inspirational thoughts. Sometimes Miss Prawn rummaged through books of sermons and poetry to find things to copy down. Sometimes she thought up her own. But *The Reveries of Madeline Prawn* was part of her hard-working life as well, because it was full of lists of things to be done *today*. She would consult her list and run from one thing to the next, hurrying back to the book on her desk to check off each item with a dashing stroke of the pen. Oh, the day was too short to get everything done! Miss Prawn got up early, terribly early, ridiculously early, to squeeze more accomplishments into every passing day.

This morning the first item on her list was

Plant Flowers

So Miss Prawn was planting flowers.

The flowers were white roses. She had bought them in the dime store the day before. They were all exactly alike, long stiff sprays with green plastic stems and white plastic blossoms.

It was five o'clock in the morning. The sky was still gray, only a little rosy at one side. The grass was wet. Nothing daunted, Miss Prawn put on her galoshes, took down her garden fork and iron rake from their new hooks on the wall of her garage, stuck a trowel in her pocket, and attacked the front yard.

She had already marked out a rectangle in the lawn. Now Miss Prawn forked out clods of wet grass and broke up the dirt underneath. Then she smoothed the dirt with the rake. At last she got down on her knees and began planting her plastic flowers with the trowel.

The child from the house next door gave her a turn.

Miss Prawn dropped her trowel. "Go away, little girl," she said.

Georgie was struck dumb. Her face flushed with embarrassment. Her feet were stuck to the ground.

Miss Prawn shook her head in irritation and picked up her trowel. "Oh, dear, now I suppose I've hurt your feelings. But look here, it's nothing against you personally. It's just that I don't like children. I mean, it's just part of my personality. Everybody has their own personal tastes. Some people don't like olives. Or fish. It's just the way they are. I myself don't happen to care for children. I mean, it's really not your fault."

Georgie nodded without a word and melted away into her own front yard. A moment later she was running down Walden Street with the wind at her back.

8

THE KIND INTERFERENCE OF MR. PREEK

*I*T SEEMED SENSIBLE to Georgie, what Miss Prawn had said. People liked things and they didn't like things. Miss Prawn didn't like children. She, Georgie, was a child. She would try not to offend Miss Prawn. From now on she would stay out of Miss Prawn's sight as well as she could.

Georgie clumped in her rubber boots past the police station and the row of young maple trees that grew beside the road. The leafy heads of the trees were rumpled in the wind. The field across from the police station was full of enormous cabbages. Packing boxes for the cabbages were stacked beside the road. Georgie half ran and half blew past the maple trees and the cabbages and the cabbage boxes. Then she slowed down as the flat road began to go uphill beyond the high school. Sturdily Georgie walked up the hill. At last she came to Route 2. The traffic light hanging over the highway was red. There were no cars coming in either direction, because it was too early for the morning rush of cars to Boston. But Georgie waited patiently for the light to turn green, and then she galloped across the wide four-lane highway and stalked along the road beside the woods on the other side.

As she walked, she listened to her boots. Each boot made two noises at every step, one when the foot inside the boot came down, and another when the rubber toe came down. *Ka-bump, ka-bump, ka-bump, ka-bump.* Georgie strode along firmly. She wasn't tired. There wasn't enough flesh on her light bones to weigh her down. She felt she could tramp onward steadfastly forever.

But perhaps she should stop for a snack. The smell of the peanut-butter sandwich in the bib pocket of her overalls was making her hungry. She would save the sandwich, but perhaps she could eat her banana right now. Georgie sat down on the dusty grass beside the road and peeled the banana and ate it slowly. Then she stuffed the peel in her pocket and reached out idly for a fat blade of grass. Putting it between her thumbs, she blew on it. *Hoot, hoot* went the grass.

A dog barked. Was it a dog? Georgie looked up. No, no, it was the swans. Not swans, geese! They were coming back! They must be flying back from Walden Pond. Flying away! Oh, oh, she had missed them!

Georgie flung up her arms to say, *Wait, wait.*

A-WARK, a-WARK! hooted the geese, flapping over Georgie's head, over the pine trees in the woods. And then, once again, the last goose in the flock fell back and veered away and dropped out of the sky toward Georgie. He was coming, he was coming again! It was the Goose Prince!

Georgie's lifted face shone in the flat rays of the rising sun. Once again the great bird hovered over her, looking down at her with his round black eyes, making some sort of warble in his throat. She could see the delicate white edgings and the soft shadings of the gray feathers on his breast. She could feel the breath of his flapping wings on her forehead!

But then the goose was startled once again. A car was squealing its brakes beside Georgie, jerking to a stop, and the driver was beeping his horn in loud blasts.

Georgie's goose flew away. He flew straight up over the trees and disappeared, racing after the rest of the flock in the direction of Nine Acre Corner.

Georgie's face twisted with disappointment. She

dropped her arms and turned to look at the car. A man was jumping out, running up to her.

"Are you all right, little girl?" He was bending down, the round gray mass of his face filling all the world.

Georgie stared up at him dumbly, tears running down her cheeks.

"That big duck, he was attacking you, didn't you see? It's a good thing I came along and had the presence of mind to honk my horn. A fine thing, when a little child isn't safe on the streets of Concord. I just wish I had a gun."

"No, no," sobbed Georgie.

"Just get in my car now, honey, and I'll take you home." The man still towered over Georgie. His hat and coat were made of fuzzy fur. The fur was shiny with tiny glittering fibers. His face was so close Georgie could see the black coarse lopped hairs on his chin. His cheeks were like the whitish-gray clay she made from flour and salt.

Georgie didn't want to get in his car. She shook her head and backed away. But the man put his arm around her shoulders and bundled her into the back seat.

"You're Fred Hall's little stepdaughter, isn't that right?" he said. "I thought so. I must say, I'm surprised Fred would let his little girl run around all over the place, crossing a big highway all by herself at this hour in the morning. Mind your own business, I always say, but just the same I'm a little surprised."

The man was Mr. Preek. Georgie had seen him in his bank on Thoreau Street. She was afraid of him. She huddled in the back seat and looked at the plump creases on the back of his neck as he zoomed his car across Route 2. Then she looked away from Mr. Preek and stared blankly out the window.

Ralph Preek would have been astonished to know that Georgie was afraid of him. Unlike his secretary, Madeline Prawn, Mr. Preek loved children. Well-behaved children. Polite, well-brought-up children. Chubby children with pink cheeks and golden hair. *I am the sort of man who loves children*, Mr. Preek often said to himself. And whenever his customers brought their children into his bank, he would open the gate that separated his desk from the windows of the tellers and stroll up to the children, beaming, and pat their heads and hand them lollipops. Some of the children would say thank you. They were the good children. Others would stop up their mouths with the lollipops and stare back at him sullenly. They were the bad ones. And then Mr. Preek's generosity would turn sour, and he would go back to his desk in silent scorn.

Now, looking in the rearview mirror at the small child in the back seat of his car, he felt the same disdain

rising in his breast. The child was pitiful, a poor speci-
men, all skin and bone and lank pale hair. Just look at
the way she was staring out the window with her lower
lip hanging slack! She was probably stupid. You could
always tell. She might even be retarded. It would serve
Fred Hall right to have a backward child. The man was
infuriating. Fascinating and infuriating at the same time.
Oh, everybody always thought he was so clever, keeping
a school! Calling it a *college*! When it was just a bunch of
ragged tatterdemalions hanging around Fred Hall's front
porch, pretending to be *graduate students*. As if that big
ugly house on Walden Street were an accredited univer-
sity. Which it wasn't. Oh, it made Mr. Preek so mad. And
the place wasn't even solvent. The school wasn't making
any money. As Fred Hall's personal banker, Ralph Preek
knew that solid fact better than anyone else. And then,
of course, as if the poor fool hadn't been in deep enough
trouble already, Fred had gone and burdened himself
with a family. He had married that widow-woman with
the retarded child. Oh, the mess some people made of
their lives!

Mr. Preek pulled his car up in front of Georgie's
house and got out. He could have saved time by dropping the child on the sidewalk and driving away. But he
wanted credit where credit was due. Shrewdly he sus-
pected that Georgie might say nothing to her family

about the kind man who had saved her life. Squeezing her delicate fingers tightly in his fat hand, he walked her up to the front porch and rang the bell.

But Eddy was just opening the door. Eddy was on his way to school with his knapsack on his back. Eddy took one look and shouted over his shoulder, "Here she is. Georgie's back."

Aunt Alex came running, her face flooded with relief. "Oh, Georgie dear," she said, "thank goodness." Then she recovered herself and smiled her ordinary motherly smile. "Did you find the swans?"

Georgie shook her head miserably. Tugging her hand free from Mr. Preek's grasp, she slipped in the door. The gloomy depths of the front hall swallowed her up.

Aunt Alex and Eddy were left alone with the bulky object on the front porch.

Mr. Preek was feeling neglected. "I just wanted to be sure, Mrs. Hall, that the child was all right. I mean, the poor little thing had such a scare out there on the road."

"A scare?" Aunt Alex put her hand to her mouth. "Georgie? Was it a car?"

"No, no, not a car. A duck. A giant duck attacked her from the sky."

"A *duck*?" said Eddy in disbelief.

"It attacked her?" Aunt Alex stared at Mr. Preek, and then she smiled. "Oh, surely not."

"I was there," said Mr. Preek. "I saw the whole thing." He frowned through the door at the white bust beside the stairs. The bust gazed back at him solemnly, and for a moment Mr. Preek was transfixed and almost forgot where he was. Then he blinked and shifted his eyes to the threadbare fringe of the parlor curtain. "I tell you, Mrs. Hall, I saw it with my own eyes. I was a witness. If I hadn't come along at that very moment and honked my horn, the bird would have knocked her down. Or snatched her up into the sky and carried her away. You hear about such things. But fortunately, by a stroke of luck, I just happened to be passing by. Quick as a wink, I knew what to do, and I honked my horn. It flew away. It was a whole flock. There were several hundred giant ducks."

"Giant ducks!" Eddy giggled. He edged around Mr. Preek and clattered down the porch steps.

"Well, I don't know," murmured Aunt Alex vaguely, staring past Mr. Preek, turning to watch Eddy jog around the corner onto Everett Street.

Mr. Preek was shocked. The woman wasn't taking the matter seriously! "Does Fred own a gun?" he said. "Look here, I'm going to get a gun myself. We can't have little children attacked on the streets of our own hometown. Something's got to be done."

"Oh, but you shouldn't," said Aunt Alex, putting out her hand. "Oh, I don't think—"

But Mr. Preek was turning away. He was lifting his puffy hand in farewell. "Oh, it's nothing at all, Mrs. Hall. Don't thank me."

Aunt Alex closed the door softly. "I didn't," she said.

9

THE GEORGIE PROTECTION
SOCIETY

N OW, GEORGIE DEAR," said Uncle Freddy, "what's
all this about a giant duck?"

Supper was over. Uncle Freddy and Eddy
were doing the dishes. Uncle Freddy was washing the
pots and pans, Eddy was drying the silverware, chuck-
ing forks into a drawer. Eleanor and Aunt Alex and
Georgie were doing a puzzle on the kitchen table. The
puzzle was a picture of the Bay of Naples, with a vol-
cano erupting in one corner. Most of the pieces were the
same color, blue water or blue sky.

"It wasn't a giant duck," said Georgie. "It was a
swan. Oh, no! I mean a goose." Then Georgie jumped up
from the kitchen table and ran to the window. A moth

was fluttering up and down the window screen. "It was the Goose Prince," said Georgie. "He wants to be my friend." The screen came up with a jerk. The moth darted into the kitchen and began thumping its soft body against the shade of the lamp hanging over the table.

Aunt Alex stirred the pieces of the puzzle in the box. "A prince? A goose prince? He wasn't going to hurt you, was he, Georgie?"

"Oh, no." Georgie was shocked. She slammed down the screen. "You know what?" Plumping herself down at the table again, Georgie beamed at her mother. "I think he wants to teach me how to fly."

"Oh, Georgie, there you go again." Eleanor looked meaningfully at Eddy.

Eddy hurled the dish towel at the towel rack and rolled his eyes at Eleanor. "Oh, come on now, Georgie," he said, sitting down beside Eleanor, jabbing her in the ribs with his elbow.

"Ouch," said Eleanor, jabbing him back. But she knew what his elbow meant. He was reminding her of their new agreement, their secret pact. Eleanor and Eddy had organized a new club, the Georgie Protection Society. It had a membership of two. Its whole purpose was to help Georgie, because the poor little kid didn't seem to be able to help herself. The Georgie Protection

Society would keep her from doing queer things. It would help her grow up to be all right. Normal, like other people. Not crazy and a little bit weird.

"Flying again, eh?" said Eddy, giving Georgie a friendly poke. "What a crazy little kid!"

Georgie smiled at Eddy and said nothing. Then she hooked together two blue puzzle pieces, and two more.

Eddy watched the puzzle fall swiftly into place under Georgie's clever fingers. It was funny the way she made him feel. She was only his stepcousin, after all, but for some reason he wanted to do things for her. He didn't know why. He certainly didn't feel that way about his sister Eleanor. Eleanor could take care of herself—altogether too well! Being the brother of Eleanor meant you had to be on your guard all the time, and grab the best half of something before Eleanor grabbed it herself. But it was different with Georgie. Georgie didn't know how to grab. She just took whatever was left over. She didn't stick up for herself at all. And now she seemed to be in some kind of funny trouble. So they had decided to do something. They didn't know what. They were going to keep their eyes and ears open. They would wait and see.

Uncle Freddy was sitting down at the table, completing the family circle. "So it's flying again, is that it, Georgie dear?" he said. "Are you sure, dear heart, that you really want to fly? Don't you think it is happiness enough to walk freely on the ground?"

Georgie smiled back confidently at Uncle Freddy. "Oh, but I already know how to fly. I mean, I think I do. I mean, I think I can a little bit." Georgie's face blanched. Her mouth turned blue around the edges. The moth battered itself weakly against the lampshade, and then it fell to the table and keeled over on its back. Georgie was transfixed by doubt. Could she fly or couldn't she? Deftly she reached out and tipped the moth right side up, and then she rose from the table and slipped out into the hall.

Eleanor shook her head as the door closed softly behind Georgie. "You know what Georgie needs? A friend. She should have friends her own age to play with. She needs to get her mind off flying." Eleanor scowled at Aunt Alex. "I'll tell you what I'll do. I'll ask somebody over myself. You know that little girl who lives right around the corner on Laurel Street? Dorothea Broom?"

Eddy recoiled in horror. "Oh, no, not Dorothea. Georgie doesn't want to play with creepy little Dorothea Broom."

"Now, look," said Eleanor. "Think about it. What if Georgie decides to fly off the roof?" Staring fiercely at Eddy, Eleanor pounded her fist on the table. The

56

puzzle jumped and came apart. One of the cats leaped off Aunt Alex's lap and skittered across the floor. And then Eleanor stopped, frightened by her own question, remembering John Green. John Green had fallen off the roof a couple of years ago. It had been terrible. Horrible. He had recovered at last, but the whole thing had been ghastly. Absolutely ghastly.

Eddy winced and closed his eyes. Eddy remembered John Green better than anybody. How could he ever forget? "Well, all right. Go ahead and invite somebody over. But not Dorothea. Not gruesome little goody-goody Dorothea Broom."

"Now, listen, Eleanor dear," said Aunt Alex, "don't do anything yet. Just be patient. Not yet. Just wait."

The bronze figure on the newel post was lighting up the front hall, just as usual, casting a warm radiance over the stair carpet and the white bust of Henry Thoreau and the faded wallpaper and the picture of the clipper ship over the piano.

Georgie hesitated beside the white bust of Henry in the curve of the stairs. If he were alive, would he like children? Yes, decided Georgie, he would. And anyway, he *was* alive, even though he didn't get down off his tall stand and move around like other people. He was awake inside his marble whiteness. He was listening. He could hear what went on around him, Georgie was sure of that. She turned away, then glanced back at him quickly, trying to catch him off guard, hoping to see him yawn or blink or turn his head to look at her. But he was still gazing straight ahead at the wall in front of him.

Georgie went up close to Henry and stared into his marble eyes. They were wonderful eyes, so real! In the middle of each eye a ring had been carved, and in the center of the ring there was a deep hole. Henry's eyes looked big and sparkling and alive. Georgie moved closer still, until her nose was brushing Henry's, until his eyes melted away and gazed vaguely right through her, right through her own eyes and her own brain and out the back of her head and through the wall of the house and through the walls of all the other houses. Uncle Freddy said Henry was looking all the way across fields and highway and woods, all the way to Walden Pond and the stone posts where his house used to be. The question that was on Georgie's mind spilled over, and she murmured, "Henry, do you think I can fly?" Then she backed away, and Henry's eyes came into focus again. He looked amiable and friendly. *Yes*, he seemed to be saying. *Yes, Georgie, you certainly can.*

Georgie turned away and stalked to the front door. But what if she had only dreamed it? And that big jump yesterday from the front porch, what if that was all it was, a big jump and nothing more, like Eddy's huge crashing leap from the front-hall stairs?

Putting an anxious hand on the knob of the front door, Georgie went out on the porch. She stood at the top of the steps and stared down at the cement walk in front of her.

In the kitchen they were still talking about Georgie.

"She's such a sober little person," said Uncle Freddy, shaking his head. "When she gets an idea into her little noggin . . ."

"I know," said Aunt Alex, looking at him solemnly. "She holds fast."

10

MISS PRAWN BEHOLDS
A MIRACLE

*I*N THE HOUSE NEXT DOOR, Madeline Prawn was sitting at her desk, feeling cozily surrounded by her things. Her front room was chockful of furniture and ornaments, lumped and puffed and cluttered around Miss Prawn in a padded kind of cushiony order. Flat things were fancy with doilies and cloths and shawls. Round things were fluffy with crocheted covers and embroidered scarves. The tufted chairs and overstuffed sofas were mounded with pillows. The tables were crowded with pictures and knickknacks. Gold jars of gilded cattails and ostrich plumes stood here and there. On the mantel squatted an immense purple pincushion stabbed with antique hat pins. And in front of the window an enormous fern on a wicker stand blocked out the soft light of evening.

But it didn't block it out altogether. Around the edges of the fern Miss Prawn had Seen Something.

She had been watering the fern. She had stood staring out the window for a moment with the watering can in her hand, and then she had put it down and darted to her writing desk.

Miss Prawn's book of reveries was lying open on the desk. At the top of the page was her inspirational quotation for the day:

You must wake and call me early, call me early, mother dear. . . .

—ALFRED, LORD TENNYSON

Under the quotation was a reminder to do something the next day:

Tomorrow: dig a shrub border along the property line. Plant sharp things, spiny things, thorny things. The children next door don't seem to know where their yard ends and mine begins.

1. Dagger plant?

2. Sword bush?

3. Roses with giant thorns?

If this barrier fails to keep them out, I will be forced to speak to their parents (or guardians, or whatever mixed-up relations those people are to each other). I'll simply explain that I really don't care for children.

But now Miss Prawn had lost interest in her book of reveries. She pushed it aside with trembling fingers and snatched up her pen and began driving it wildly across a clean sheet of paper. She was writing a letter to her employer, Mr. Ralph Preek, president of the Thoreau Street Bank.

Dear Ralph,

I write in haste about a matter of supreme impor-tance. Since my telephone has not yet been connected, I will send this by special messenger.

I have just witnessed a miracle. Oh Ralph, it is vouchsafed to few of us to behold such things!

The child next door is a SAINT.

Either that, or she is a visitor from FAIRY-LAND.

Believe me, Ralph, cross my heart and hope to die.

Far be it from me to let a fib or the tiniest little white lie cross my lips. THIS IS THE NAKED TRUTH.

A moment ago I happened to glance out the window, and I tell you, Ralph, I nearly fell to the floor in a swoon. She was FLYING. She had climbed up on the railing of the front porch (this is Fred Hall's youngest, that skinny little stepdaughter), and then she jumped, and believe me, Ralph, I hope to die, she went up in the air as high as the roof and then came down easy and landed on the grass. It was a genuine bona fide guaranteed miracle, and think of it, Ralph, it was vouchsafed to me, Madeline Prawn, to stand here and behold it. I swear this is the truth. What have I done, I said to myself, to deserve this blessing. Oh, unknown to us in our humbleness, Ralph, I said to myself, how our inner goodness works in mysterious ways on the Almighty Deep.

Of course on the other hand perhaps she is a fairy moon-child. You must know, Ralph, I mean it is a well-known fact that fairies come at the full of the moon and kidnap a newborn babe and leave one of their own in its place and then one day at the full of the moon the moon-child flies away to join the fairies and is gone forever. That is a fact. A scientific fact. You see them every now and again, you know, Ralph. These weird children. Odd little creatures. Peculiar. And I must say this little girl next door really fills the bill. She is certainly strange. You know what I mean. Big eyes, skinny little toothpick legs. Hair without any color to it. Skin like blue milk. That kind of child. And oh, Ralph, doesn't it make your blood boil to think that somewhere out there in fairyland there may be a healthy pink-cheeked darling lost to the world forever because of this little GNOME?

So you see, Ralph, we must get together and talk. There are things that might be done. Who knows where such a piece of good fortune might lead? Having been vouchsafed the witnessing of this miracle, I have a responsibility to myself and what's more, dear Ralph, just think of it, TO THE WORLD AT LARGE.

I am thinking, for instance (just to get the ball rolling), of filling small bottles with water and having them blessed by the young saint. We could offer them for sale. A healing elixir.

This is the sort of thing you do with saints.

Or we could even consider a more practical enterprise like renting out parking lots from which the child's ascents might be observed. The possibilities are ENDLESS.

Breathlessly,
Madeline

Miss Prawn put down her pen and read her letter over. Astonished by the force of her own words, she felt suddenly very pious and very rich. It felt wonderful to be both of those things at the same time. Miss Prawn stuck the letter in an envelope and scrawled on the outside *RUSH RUSH: Deliver at once to Mr. Ralph Preek.* Then she hurried out-of-doors with the letter in her hand, crossed Laurel Street, and knocked on the door of the first house.

A little girl opened the door and looked up at Miss Prawn.

Miss Prawn inspected the little girl with sharp attention. Now, if it had been at all possible for Miss Prawn to like children, she might have become fond of this one, because the child looked the way children were *supposed* to look, plump and pink with a rosebud mouth and yellow curly hair.

"How would you like to earn a quarter, Dorothea?" said Miss Prawn.

11

DOROTHEA BRINGS
THE WORD

RALPH PREEK WAS DOZING IN front of his TV set after supper when he was awakened by the barking of dogs in his front yard. He rushed to the window. Two half-grown German shepherds were bounding through his perennial border, trampling his prize chrysanthemums.

Mr. Preek threw up the sash and shouted at the dogs, but they went right on frisking among his flowers, knocking the giant blossoms this way and that, snapping the tall stems. He rushed outside, remembering, too late, his resolve to buy a gun. A duck gun! It would come in handy for emergencies like this. A little spray of buckshot, and these dogs would never come back. They would have learned their lesson. "Get out," he shouted at the top of his lungs. "Get out, out, out!"

The dogs stopped tumbling over each other in his flower bed and looked at him in surprise. Then they lunged the whole length of the chrysanthemum border, barking, and raced away up the street. Mr. Preek ran after them, gasping, and then he slowed down and stopped, to look at the little girl who was marching up the sidewalk.

It was a nice little girl in a pretty dress. Her hair was yellow. Her cheeks were chubby. Why, it was little Dorothea Broom. Mr. Preek had often given Dorothea a lollipop when she came into the bank with her mother. She had always said thank you so nicely! Mr. Preek's anger cooled. How he loved little children!

Dorothea walked straight up to him and stopped. "This is for you," she said, holding up an envelope. "From Miss Prawn."

"Why, thank you, dear child." Mr. Preek took the letter. Dorothea's chubby cheeks grew chubbier. And then she curtsied. She did! She curtsied like a lady-in-waiting at the Court of St. James's!

Mr. Preek was stunned. He gave Dorothea a dollar. Then he went inside and read Miss Prawn's letter and sat down at the kitchen table to write a reply. Dorothea waited outside, pressing her nose against the screen door.

My dear Madeline, [wrote Mr. Preek]

There are no such things as miracles. The child is in the power of a very large duck. Only this morning I beheld a similar event. I believe it is an example of that peculiar attraction by which beasts of the lower orders exert dominion over other creatures in mysterious ways. You are familiar, I am sure, with the cobra, which can freeze its victim into immobility by some sort of powerful hypnotism. And you must have heard of animal magnetism. Surely these forces explain this phenomenon. The duck simply PULLED the child into the air. This morning I drove it away before it could snatch her up in its claws or draw her up from the ground by the force of magnetic attraction. She is a very small child, you will remember, almost weightless, compared to the immense size and wingspread of the giant bird. The creature is a menace to hearth and home and must be destroyed.

Do nothing till you hear from me.

Yours truly,
Ralph

Then Mr. Preek wrote Miss Prawn's name on the envelope and handed the letter to Dorothea Broom.

Dorothea smiled again.

Why, the child had dimples! A delicious pair of dimples, one in the middle of each chubby pink cheek! Mr. Preek gave Dorothea another dollar.

12

AT LAST

*I*T WAS BEDTIME. Georgie put on her pajamas, pulled
back the covers of her bed, laid Dollabella on the
pillow, and climbed in beside her. Then she adjusted
the blankets carefully so that they came up only as far
as Dollabella's chin (or as far as the place where
Dollabella's chin would have been, if Dollabella had had
a chin). Then Georgie turned off the light beside the bed
and lay back on her pillow and stared up at the dark,
smiling.

Her smile stretched from the closet on one side of
the room to the window on the other, she was so glad.

She had flown. There was no doubt at all. She had
drifted up to the top of the house, and then she had floated

to the ground, coming to rest on the grass in the front yard like a feather or a piece of milkweed down. . . .

So when the Goose Prince came for her, Georgie was ready.

His gentle hooting woke her before dawn. The sound was like a blade of grass trembling between her thumbs. Georgie cocked her head up from the pillow, instantly alert, her body tense with listening. *Tap-tap.* He was tapping lightly with his beak against the glass.

Eagerly Georgie slipped out of bed and pattered across the floor.

The Goose Prince was standing on the porch roof, his long neck erect, the narrow crescent moon cocked behind his head. Soon the sky would be glimmering with morning.

Georgie lifted the window. The sash slid easily to the top. She could feel herself beaming, pieces of happiness flying off her face to the quiet trees and the sleeping houses and the empty road. "Oh, hello there," whispered Georgie.

The Goose Prince was a little comical, seen close up. His long beak was like a big nose, and his two round eyes bulged a little away from his head. His webbed feet turned in like a pigeon's. He spoke, and it was like a flute talking. His voice was a little husky, like the note of the blade of grass.

71

"Would you like to fly around the pond?" said the Goose Prince.

"Oh, yes!" Georgie climbed out the window and stood on the roof of the porch, gripping the shingles with her bare feet, shivering a little in the night air. Then she turned quickly around, reached back through the window, and pulled Eddy's jacket from the back of the rocking chair.

The Goose Prince stood stock-still, waiting for her. He was smiling. His beak didn't turn up at the corners like the smile of a person, but Georgie could tell that he was pleased. Perhaps he was as glad as she was—and that was very glad! Now he was turning around awkwardly and bending down. Georgie climbed on his back. It was cushiony and soft, but there was a hard feeling of strong muscles beneath the feathers. At first Georgie sat upright with her legs folded under her. But that didn't feel right. The Goose Prince waited patiently while she tried lying forward and tucking her head into the space between the base of his throat and his left wing.

There, that was better. Georgie locked her thin arms gently around his chest. Now her knees fitted perfectly behind his wings.

The Goose Prince curved his neck and looked back at her kindly. "Are you all right now?" he said.

"I'm fine," said Georgie.

"Well, then, hold on tight," said the Goose Prince.

And then he took off. Clumsily he slithered down the sloping shingles and sprang off the edge of the roof, flapping heavily over the bushes. Georgie could feel the brave cry choking in his throat as the great buckets of his wings caught the air and hurled it downward. His body was rocking up, up, up, flapping and rising. Georgie rocked with it and clung with all her might. They were lifting, lifting, straight up over the house to the top of the chimney. For a moment they were poised over the steep intersecting roofs of Georgie's house, and she could look down past the house next door and see the white flowers in Miss Prawn's front yard.

"Oh!" said Georgie. Miss Prawn had finished her flowery message. Her plastic rose garden said

WELCOME TO CONCORD

But now Miss Prawn's house and Georgie's house were tipping backward as the Goose Prince stretched his long black neck and began flying in the direction of the highway. Lying on his back, Georgie could feel the rapid thump of her excited heart against the flexing pull of his wings. Together they were like a single engine throbbing smoothly through the air.

She was filled with delight. The wind blew her hair

streaming away from her face, it rippled the hems of her pajamas, and it breathed cool on her bare feet as she lay like a feather between the churning wings, looking down at the houses rushing away below her. Walden Street was a long gray ribbon, turning and bending on its way to Route 2. She could see the flat top of the police station, she could see Laurel Street, she could see Dorothea's house. It looked as small as a dollhouse. And the people inside would be tiny too, Mr. Broom and Mrs. Broom and Mary Jane and Dorothea. They would be like dolls, with perfect little fingers and toes. Rushing high over the house on the back of the Goose Prince, Georgie felt as if she could reach down with her giant hands and take off the roof of the house and pick up Dorothea and say, "Okay now, Dorothea, time to get up," and prop her in a kitchen chair like a doll.

The houses were gone. The Goose Prince was flying on steadily over the cabbage fields. The air blowing in Georgie's face had risen cool and moist from the boggy place in the woods. It smelled of cabbages growing in wet earth. It was spicy with the scent of a hundred thousand leaves in the Town Forest. And there was a musky smell too, from a fox that still lived in the forest. (Georgie didn't know about the fox. She only knew the air smelled fresh and a little wild.)

The flight didn't last long. Already the Goose Prince

was descending in a long glide over the highway toward Walden Pond. Already she could see the tops of the pine trees in the woods around the water. And then at the last minute, Georgie glanced back over her shoulder at the town of Concord. Her hair was blowing over her face, the buildings were half hidden by the puffy trees, but Georgie thought she saw for just a second the dark windows of her own house visible above the trees, far away. The whole house is asleep, thought Georgie. They are all asleep, breathing sigh, sigh, and their breath blows the curtains in the windows, and the curtains are floating out white, and my mother and Uncle Freddy are in there sound asleep, and they don't know I'm flying! flying! up here in the sky!

"Oh, bring her back safe," murmured Aunt Alex, standing behind the curtain, gazing at the small moving spot that was Georgie flying in front of the crescent moon.

13

EDDY KEEPS HIS EYES AND EARS OPEN

O N WEEKDAYS THE Thoreau Street Bank closed its doors promptly at three in the afternoon. Usually Ralph Preek stayed at his desk working diligently until five o'clock, but today he slipped out with the last of his customers and made his way to Macone's Sporting Goods Store on Lowell Road.

Mr. Preek was entirely unaware of Georgie's miraculous flight before dawn on the back of the Goose Prince, but the enormous bird and the little girl were both very much on his mind.

"What can I do for you?" said the man behind the counter, spreading his hands wide on the glass case of jackknives and fishing lures and looking at Mr. Preek.

There was only one other customer in the store, a red-headed boy examining a shelf of model rockets and airplanes.

"I would like to purchase a gun," said Mr. Preek.

"What kind of gun do you want?"

"Something large and powerful. For large waterfowl. Giant ducks." Clearing his throat, Mr. Preek introduced himself. (His name ought to mean something, after all: *Ralph Alonzo Preek, the president of the Thoreau Street Bank.*)

The eyes of the man behind the counter failed to blink with recognition. "Ducks?" he said. "Oh, you don't want anything too powerful if you're going duck hunting. This one here would be about right. Twelve-gauge. Pump-action. Three shots and you load again."

"Hmmmm," said Mr. Preek. He took the gun and fiddled with the trigger. "Looks kind of feeble to me. I tell you, this bird is gigantic. Dangerous. Attacking little children on the streets of Concord."

"Attacking children? Oh, you must mean somebody's barnyard Toulouse goose. I had a flock once myself. They sometimes run out and peck at strangers."

The redheaded boy put a long narrow box on the counter. *Assemble your own PHOSPHORESCENT MOON ROCKET X-100*, said the label on the box. "I'll take this one," said the boy.

"No, no," said Mr. Preek, "this is a wild bird, I tell you. It descends from the air and snatches little children. I saw it with my own eyes."

"Is that so?" The man behind the counter looked doubtfully at Mr. Preek. Then he rang up the boy's money in the cash register and put the rocket model in a paper bag. "Well, I don't know. Anyway, that's the kind of gun you want if you're going after any kind of ducks or geese. Have you got a license? And you can't shoot anything now, you know that? The season doesn't begin for a couple of weeks."

"A couple of weeks?" Mr. Preek was indignant. "But the matter is urgent. I'll speak to the selectmen."

"Not the selectmen. That wouldn't do any good. You'll have to go to the State House in Boston. It's a Massachusetts state law."

"The governor then. I'll go straight to the governor."

"Well, lots of luck. You want this gun or not?"

"I'll take it," said Ralph Preek.

The boy left the store with his paper bag and started home. Along the road beside the supermarket, the September sunlight struck the shiny leaves of the pokeweed bushes, bouncing off them as from so many glittering mirrors. But Eddy saw nothing but the black pavement in front of him and his own advancing feet.

Mr. Preek was buying a duck gun. Because of

Georgie. Mr. Preek was trying to protect Georgie from the attack of a giant duck. But it wasn't a duck, it was a Canada goose. It was Georgie's goose, the one that wanted to be her friend. But of course Georgie was crazy. The goose didn't want to be Georgie's friend. It was just an ordinary goose in a great big flock of Canada geese. It had just happened to come down near the place where Georgie was. Crazy little old Georgie. She needed protecting, all right, and that was a fact. But not by Mr. Preek. The Georgie Protection Society could take care of Georgie perfectly well, without any outside help from big fat bossy men with guns, like Mr. Ralph Preek.

Eddy turned in at the gate of No. 40 Walden Street and started up the steps of the front porch, calling, "Georgie, hey, Georgie." Then he had to step aside, because people were pouring out the door, Millicent O'Toole and Arthur Hathaway and all the rest. They all said hello to Eddy and ambled down the porch steps, laughing and talking. Classes were over for the day. They were all going home.

"Here I am, Eddy," said Georgie. She wasn't in the house. She was standing up in the bushes, smiling up at Eddy through arching boughs of forsythia.

"Oh, there you are, Georgie." Eddy ran down the steps and crawled into the bushes and squatted down beside her. "Listen here, Georgie, I want to know what that goose was like. I mean, what did he *really* do? You know, that big goose you saw yesterday morning."

Georgie smiled down at Dollabella. Carefully she picked up a maple leaf heaped with blades of grass and red berries from the hedge in front of the house. "Here, Eddy, have some lettuce and tomato salad?"

"Gee, thanks." Eddy took a berry and squished it between his fingers.

Georgie stirred her air-tea in its acorn cup with a twig and took a sip. She couldn't stop smiling. In the hour before dawn the Goose Prince had carried her three times around Walden Pond, skimming the tops of the pine trees, and then he had brought her safely home, secretly, silently. In plenty of time for breakfast. In plenty of time for school. It had been wonderful, a dream come true, a dream that was real. Georgie looked at Eddy. She didn't know what to say. It wouldn't be right to lie, not to Eddy. But it was all right anyway—Eddy was talking about yesterday morning, when Mr. Preek had frightened the Goose Prince away—not about today.

"He was nice. He was coming down. Over there by the woods. By the highway. It was right between the woods and the highway."

"But he wasn't coming down just to see *you*?"

"To see me?" Georgie paused and thought it over.

"Well, yes, he was. He was really nice! And then that man honked his horn, and the Goose Prince—I mean, the goose—flew away."

"He was just coming down, that's all, and then he flew away? Well, where did Mr. Preek get the idea he was dangerous? I saw him just now, Mr. Preek, I mean. He was buying—"

And then it was Eddy's turn to hold something back. He stood up. "Say, Georgie, you want to see something? Come on inside. I've got a new plastic model to put together. It's a moon rocket. It glows in the dark. Come on, I'll show you."

"It glows in the dark? It *does*?" Georgie couldn't believe it.

But in the stuffy narrow space behind the coats in the closet under the stairs, the hundreds of little plastic pieces of Eddy's rocket ship glowed softly in the velvet dark, an eerie luminous green. "Isn't that great?" said Eddy.

"Wow," breathed Georgie.

"Wait till I put the whole thing together," said Eddy.

The doorbell rang. Eddy fumbled through the coats, opened the closet door, and went out into the front hall.

Georgie looked timidly out of the closet.

It was Miss Prawn, Miss Madeline Prawn, the new neighbor who didn't like children. Quickly Georgie ducked back into the closet.

But Miss Prawn had seen Georgie. Hungrily she looked past Eddy at the closet door. Miss Prawn was carrying two big empty plastic jugs. She was smiling and smiling and showing her teeth. "Might I have some water, young man? My faucets have stopped working."

14

MISS PRAWN AND THE SAINTLY CHILD

"YOUR FAUCETS HAVE stopped working?" Eddy was surprised. "That's funny."

"I know," said Miss Prawn. "But they did. They stopped. Not a drop from a single faucet in the house." She cocked her head sideways and stared past Eddy at the closet door, grinning and grinning. It looked like hard work to Eddy, the way she was stretching her face in spasmodic jerks, then stretching it some more, trying to pull her mouth sideways from its customary pursed-up spot in the middle of her face.

"Maybe you should call a plumber," he said slowly, standing smack in the middle of the doorway.

"Well, of course, of course, of course, I'll call a

83

plumber!" Miss Prawn frowned at Eddy. Then she remembered, and showed her teeth again. "But in the meantime, if I could just fill up my jugs at your kitchen sink?"

Eddy couldn't think of any reason why not. He stood aside and led the way to the kitchen. As they passed the closet door Miss Prawn's greedy eyes flashed in at Georgie. Georgie winced and turned away and pressed up against the coats. She could hear water splashing in the kitchen, going *glug-glug* into the jugs. Quickly she slipped out of the closet and hurried through the velvet curtain and hid herself in the parlor. (Georgie was just trying to be polite. Now Miss Prawn wouldn't have to look at her. Miss Prawn, who didn't like children.)

But a moment later Miss Prawn sought her out. She poked her head through the parlor curtain and stared at Georgie. Her teeth glittered roguishly. "I saw you." She chuckled. "I saw you last night on the front porch."

Georgie jerked guiltily. Miss Prawn always made her feel she had done something bad.

"I saw you jump off the front porch and fly way up in the air."

"Oh." Georgie looked around for a way to escape, but Miss Prawn was blocking the only door.

Then Miss Prawn disappeared for an instant. When

she came back through the parlor curtain she was carrying her two jugs. They were heavy with water. She thumped them on the floor. She was still beaming. "Here, dear," said Miss Prawn, pulling a piece of paper out of her pocket, "just read this out loud."

Georgie looked at the piece of paper. She rocked back and forth on her toes. She glanced shyly up at Miss Prawn and whispered, "I don't understand it."

Miss Prawn was amazed. She took the paper back and read it aloud to Georgie. "It says, OFFICIAL DOCUMENT: *I have blessed this water.* Now, sign it, dear. Just sign your name right here underneath."

Georgie looked vaguely at Miss Prawn's shoes. They were sharp-pointed shoes with fringed flaps and shoelaces and holes pricked all over the toes. Georgie pulled her chin down into her shirt and sucked the edge of her collar. Slowly she shook her head from side to side.

Miss Prawn poked something at her. "Just take this pen and sign it, I tell you, right down here at the bottom."

Georgie turned her head and gazed out the window. Fluffy pieces of milkweed were floating across the porch, drifting through the moon-shaped opening in the lattice, blowing upward and out of sight. In the meadow across the street the sun glistened on the tall stems of amber-colored grass. Georgie dropped her eyes and whispered, "No."

Miss Prawn stared at her, opening her mouth in astonishment. Why, the child couldn't write. That was the trouble. She couldn't read and she couldn't even write her own name. She must be stupid. It was pitiful. Miss Prawn thought it over shrewdly and guessed the reason why.

She was a fairy, that was it. Fairies couldn't read or write. That was a well-known fact. And just look at her. The child was certainly a fairy. (Miss Prawn narrowed her eyes and studied Georgie closely.) There were blue shadows under her eyes, and her face had a sort of skim-milk look to it. And her hair wasn't yellow or brown or any particular color. The child's hair had no more color to it than the water in the jugs. She *must* be a moon-child.

Miss Prawn gave up. She stopped smiling. Her face sagged into its usual expression of smelling something slightly unpleasant. She took an envelope out of her pocket and handed it to Georgie. "Give this to your mother, will you?" she said sharply. Then she turned on her heel and plunged through the curtain.

"Oh, wait," said Georgie, "you forgot your water." Hefting the jugs off the floor, Georgie dragged them out into the hall.

But Miss Prawn looked back at the jugs in contempt. "Never mind," she said. Marching out the front door, she yanked it shut behind her with a bang.

It was a shame about the water, thought Miss Prawn. It would have been like selling expensive perfume, only better. Think of it! Some kinds of perfume cost twenty-five dollars an ounce! And wouldn't the healing water from the Holy Well of the Saintly Child have been far more precious than the most precious and expensive perfume? Well, it had been an attractive idea. It was too bad. One hated to give it up.

The child *must* be a fairy. The evidence was all on that side.

But then again, it was still possible that she was a saint. One was caught on the horns of a dilemma. What if she *were* a saint, after all? An illiterate, ignorant, rather stupid saint? One didn't want to be overly respectful to a mere moon-child, but on the other hand (having been vouchsafed the witnessing of a genuine miracle!) one dared not be anything but nice, terribly nice, in case the poor little waif turned out to be a genuine holy bona fide saint after all.

Miss Prawn walked through her own front yard, gazing absentmindedly at the white roses that said *WELCOME TO CONCORD* in her garden of plastic flowers. She would make up her mind later on. For the present she would walk a careful line between worship on the one hand and outrage on the other.

With fairies and saints and weird abnormal creatures like that, you really had to watch your step.

15

TARGET PRACTICE

A
T THE BOTTOM OF South America there is a place of terrible heavy seas, where two oceans meet. Gathering in moving masses of water thousands of miles away, sweeping up from the South Pole in the Pacific, rolling southward from the equator in the Atlantic, opposing waves meet at last in a tremendous smash and crash of thundering crosscurrents at the tip of Cape Horn.

And yet until their climactic meeting they are nothing more than ordinary waves with schools of fish sporting in them and seabirds flying over them, ordinary waves in peaceful seas.

There can be waves like that in small inland towns

far from the ocean shore. Here and now in the town of Concord, Massachusetts, in the continent of North America, there were two such waves. Georgie and the Goose Prince were one. Ralph Alonzo Preek of the Thoreau Street Bank was the other.

On the way home from Macone's Sporting Goods Store, Mr. Preek had stopped at the Concord Library to pick up a book on the hunting of waterfowl. Now in the privacy of his own living room he took his new gun out of its box and inspected it. He oiled it and wiped it clean. He read the manual from cover to cover. Then he sat down in a comfortable chair and read aloud to himself the chapter on target exercises in his library book.

The chapter advised him to pick up his gun every now and then and point it at things at random, at the face of the clock or a picture on the wall.

. . . Now close your left eye and sight along the barrel with the right. You'll probably find you are pointing a bit over, under, or to one side or the other. Correct the hold and try again—and again and again. Before long you'll be on target every time.

Mr. Preek looked around the room. Over the mantel hung a photograph of Henry Thoreau. That would do nicely for a target. Whipping his gun up to his shoulder, he pointed it at the picture. Then, squinting one eye, he sighted along the barrel. Right on the nose! Henry Thoreau's big nose was right in the middle of the gun-sight! Pretty good for a beginner.

Grinning to himself, Mr. Preek put the gun down, picked up the book, and flipped to another chapter. Now the author was describing an exciting moment on a frozen lake during a hunting expedition with a friend.

> . . . The geese bore down on me, one slightly ahead of the other, flying straight and true at the height of about forty yards. . . . I came to my knees and poured three loads from my pump into the nearest broad white breast. In one motion I laid my gun on the ice and grabbed Ollie's. As I brought it up I saw the first bird falling, so I rammed the two loads into the other. As the last charge thumped into him, his wings folded and the two birds crashed down almost together. . . .

I'll bet I could do that, thought Mr. Preek. I could learn how. I'll be ready by the time the duck hunting season begins. I'll practice hard.

Impulsively he snatched up his gun and aimed it once again at the picture of Henry Thoreau. This time

Henry's left eye was smack in the middle of the gun-sight.

The eye looked gravely back at him.

Ralph Preek blinked. Then he lowered his gun and muttered aloud, "Well, you know how it is, old man. No offense."

16

THE CUDGEL OF FRIENDSHIP

AUNT ALEX'S AFTERNOON seminar was over. The class had been conducted in the backyard right next to the laundry line, and the sun-washed smell of the flapping shirts and billowing sheets had blown over Millicent O'Toole and Arthur Hathaway and all the rest of them, bringing a fresh homey flavor to the morning's discussion of Henry Thoreau's life at Walden Pond.

Now they were opening their lunch bags under the apple tree. Arthur was strumming his guitar. Aunt Alex picked up her books and hurried into the house by the back door.

In the kitchen she found Georgie hopping around on

one foot. Georgie stopped hopping and took something out of the bib pocket of her overalls. "This is from Miss Prawn," she said.

"Miss Prawn?" Taking the letter between finger and thumb, Aunt Alex held it at arm's length for a minute, and then she opened it thoughtfully.

Dear Mrs. Hall, [said the letter]

Far be it from me to shrink from performing my duty especially where a neighbor is concerned, because you see, Mrs. Hall, it is vouchsafed to some of us to be presented once in a lifetime with the opportunity to grant sometimes on occasion a little friendly advice and warning. In the nature of which I hereby undertake to impart the same out of a feeling of neighborly responsibility, taking up the cudgel of friendship, as it were. We go this way but once, I said to myself, and far be it from me not to interfere when I see calamity and doom and disaster coming down the pike. Speaking strictly as a neighbor, I now feel it incumbent on me to pass along to you certain pieces of information that have come my way as I have traveled along the highway of life, namely that certain things are apt to eventuate at the full of the moon. I do not wish to alarm you, but it is a well-known scientific fact. Your daughter may have been left on your

94

doorstep by the fairies at the full of the moon. If so,
then she may likewise be taken BACK by those self-
same fairies at the full of the moon. Therefore watch
out. Be on your guard. At the full of the moon keep the
child locked up. Don't say I didn't warn you. WATCH
OUT WHEN THE MOON IS FULL.

> Yours faithfully in days of trouble
> and strife, as well as in happier times,
>
> Madeline Prawn

> So I'll travel along
> With a friend and a song.
> Wilfrid Wilson Gibson

> And the song, from beginning to end,
> I found in the heart of a friend.
> Henry Wadsworth Longfellow

> Let me live in my house by the side of the road
> And be a friend of man.
> Sam Walter Foss

Aunt Alex looked up from her letter. Georgie was
gazing at her solemnly. Aunt Alex laughed.

"What does she say?" said Georgie.

"Oh, nothing," said Aunt Alex. "Just a lot of silly foolishness." Then, *rrrriiiipppp*, Georgie's mother tore Miss Prawn's letter in two and threw it in the wastebasket.

17

A Present from Georgie

THAT NIGHT THE OLD MOON was gone and the new moon wasn't born yet, so there was no moon at all. When the Goose Prince hooted softly at Georgie from the roof of the porch, there were only stars around him, sparkling through their pinholes in the blue-black sky. Joyfully Georgie hopped out of bed, snatched up Eddy's jacket, jerked it over her pajamas, threw up the window, and leaned forward into the cool night air to say hello.

Immediately the Goose Prince bent his long neck down to her in kindly greeting.

They were beak to nose. For a moment Georgie

wondered if she should kiss the Goose Prince. If she kissed him, would he turn into a real prince? But she was too shy. And, besides, she didn't want him to change into something else. He was very beautiful just the way he was.

Nimbly she clambered out the window and lay down on his back. Then the Goose Prince began working his wings, shifting his weight, churring softly in his throat. The next moment he was scrabbling down the roof with his webbed feet, beating his wings in hollow fannings, struggling upward into the air over the dew-laden grass and the dim tangle of Georgie's bush house and the dark shape of Uncle Freddy's car in the driveway and—what were those ghostly things dangling in the backyard?— the laundry, the bedspreads and the shirts and sheets, hanging wet and slack on the line. Tossing from side to side as the Goose Prince heaved himself aloft, Georgie hung on tight, and then at last the Goose Prince stretched his neck forward and settled into a steady horizontal flight. They were high over Miss Prawn's garden of plastic flowers, they were high over the dim houses, with sky above them and sky below them, and no sound but the soft buffeting of the Goose Prince's wings, gathering the air and hurling it behind him, gathering and hurling it again. Tucked close and safe on his back with her cheek pressed into the hollow between his neck and his left wing, Georgie felt the night air flow by her in running streams. Now they were over the fields, and over the highway, and over the woods, and already, looking down, Georgie could see the pond opening beneath them, flat and black below a milky film of fog.

The Goose Prince was coming down. He was going to land in the water! No longer was he choking back his hoarse cry. He was in full voice, shouting to the whole dark world of the night, *"A-WARK, a-WARK!"* He was braking his flight, bellying out his wings to slow his descent, rearing backward, dropping his black feet, catching at the water, running across it, splashing great sprays of spume to left and right. For a moment they skimmed upright across the surface like horse and rider, and then the Goose Prince sank down and settled on the water, bobbing like a cork. "Oh!" Georgie gave a small stifled cry, and pulled up her toes, shocked by the touch of the cold water. Then she let her legs fall again, and soon the water was no longer cold. Silently and serenely the Goose Prince began paddling toward the shore, moving like a ship, like a feathery galleon, stern high, bow low. Majestically he cruised northward until his breast nudged the reedy shore. Georgie could feel his feet touch bottom. Slowly the Goose Prince waded through a bristling growth of pickerelweed and gained the solid bank and climbed up on the trampled path to stand at his full height on dry ground.

Quickly Georgie hopped off his back, and then she stood respectfully at one side, wringing the water from her pajama legs, waiting to see what he would do next. The Goose Prince was waggling his tail, flapping his wings, spraying droplets of water all around, like a dog shaking itself after a swim. Then he poked his head at his back and nipped his tail feathers savagely.

Georgie waited. She looked around. They had come down in a little cove. They were standing on a curving shore. Below them the pond lay still, the mist above it thinning and vanishing. The whole luminous sky was still. Most of the stars had gone out. It was nearly dawn. Only one big star hung over the treetops, glistening, not twinkling at all. It was the same star Georgie had seen on the morning when she had set out to find the Goose Prince. Now it looked down at her enormously, one great ray falling from far away, a million miles! right into her eye. There wasn't the slightest breeze in the branches of the pine trees, only the liquid lapping of the water where they had come ashore, slapping around the stems of the bushes that grew in the water.

The Goose Prince looked kindly at Georgie. "Shall we walk up the hill?" he said.

It wasn't a big hill. Just a wide steep path up the sloping ground between the trees. They walked side by side. And then they came to a place Georgie knew.

Uncle Freddy had often brought her here. There were granite posts and a wooden sign. The posts were only gray shapes in the gray gloom of the woods, but Georgie went up to one of them and felt its stony surface. Henry Thoreau had lived here once, that was what the sign said. He had lived in a small house on the shore of Walden Pond, here where the posts were, a long time ago. Georgie smiled. If Uncle Freddy were here, he would tell her how Henry had made friends with a field mouse, how he had pulled a woodchuck out of its hole by the tail, how fishes had swum into his hand in the water, and snakes had coiled themselves around his legs. But Uncle Freddy wasn't here. Georgie said nothing.

The Goose Prince was looking at her, standing regally in the shadows, his dark neck erect. Then he yawned, stretching his bill hugely, and looked at Georgie sleepily. "Do you mind if I take a short nap?" he said.

Georgie was surprised. "Oh, no," she said. "I don't mind." Then she watched as the Goose Prince lowered himself to the ground and tucked his head into the middle of his back and closed his eyes. Sitting down beside a clump of fern, she waited for him to wake up. She didn't feel tired at all. And in a few minutes the Goose Prince lifted his head, shook himself, stood up again, and walked over to Georgie.

It made her smile, to see the way he walked. He was waddling slightly, pointing his toes in, holding his head high. But even in the dim morning light she could feel how solemn he was, and she stopped smiling.

"I want to give you something," said the Goose Prince, stopping in front of Georgie. "There's a present. I want to give you a present."

"A present?" said Georgie, startled.

Absentmindedly the Goose Prince turned and stared at the light patches of pond gleaming between the dark trunks of the trees. For a moment he seemed to have forgotten Georgie. But then he came out of his reverie and looked at her again. His face was swollen into fat bumps at either side, to show that he was smiling. "Wait," he said. "Later on. Not now."

"All right," said Georgie. But she wondered about the present. What could it be? She couldn't think of anything. And anyway what could be more wonderful than what she had already been given? Then Georgie had a guilty thought. She was suddenly overcome with the feeling that it was *she* who should be giving the present. *She* should be giving something to *him*. Oh, if only she had something to give him! Georgie put her hands in the pockets of Eddy's jacket, to feel if there was something there, pennies, or an apple, or—what would he like?—

dried kernels of corn. But there was nothing in the pockets, only the withered leftovers from Dollabella's last tea party.

But then Georgie's fingers closed on a blade of grass. She pulled it out and stretched it between her two thumbs to make a grass flute. "Listen!" she said. And then she blew.

The grass made its familiar trembling hoot. Georgie blew again. *Hoot, hoot.*

The Goose Prince opened his beak with astonishment.

Georgie blew once more on her small green flute. *Hoot, hoot. Hoot, hoot.*

The narrow face of the Goose Prince was bulging at the sides. He was beaming. "Well!" he said, "isn't that nice!"

Georgie held the blade of grass out to him on the palm of her hand. "Would you like to have it?" she said.

The Goose Prince looked at the blade of grass. Delicately he picked it up in his bill. For a minute Georgie thought he was going to eat it, but instead he lowered his head and rustled with his webbed feet in a heap of dead leaves beside one of the granite posts. He was tucking the blade of grass under the leaves. He was lifting his head. "Thank you," he said to Georgie, the fat places on each side of his head bulging more than ever. "Now are you ready?"

"Ready?" said Georgie. "Ready for what?"

But it was the very thing that was brimming in her heart. He taught her how to fly.

18

FLYYYYYYYYYY!

*T*HEY TOOK OFF FROM the pond. The ascent was not like their clumsy upward struggles from the roof of the porch at home. This time the Goose Prince made a rush forward through the water, his wings flapping, his beak open in a loud triumphant shout, *"A-WARK, a-WARK!"* At once he was aloft, with a rain of crystal drops falling from his webbed feet and streaming backward from Georgie's soaked pajama legs as they rose higher and higher over the pond. Georgie hung on tight, feeling the cold rush of air on her wet legs. Now the Goose Prince was flapping strongly over the southern shore, turning in a wide arc. Then Georgie gasped. They were not alone. There was a flock of geese below them in the water, a whole flock. They were clustered along the shore with their drowsing heads tucked into their backs, fast asleep.

"*A-WARK, a-WARK!*" As the Goose Prince shouted above them, Georgie could see heads popping up in a flurry of beating wings. She could hear a chorus of shocked croakings. *What's that? What's that? Who's there?* But then they recognized one of their own, and the wings stopped fanning. The heads sank once more into the downy backs. They all went back to sleep.

High above the slumbering flock the Goose Prince swam smoothly once again through the thick river of air. His wings were moving easily, sending pulses of the cool fragrant morning over Georgie's smiling face, lifting the lank wisps of her fine hair, blowing it backward. Below them the pine trees flung up their dark arms, as if they were pointing at Georgie—*Oh, look! Look at Georgie!* And then the Goose Prince turned his head on his long neck and gazed back at her, the dawn light shining through his bulging eyes. "Now," he said, "try it now."

At the top of the sky, clinging to him with her fingers knotted together around his throat, Georgie looked back at him, trying to understand, whispering, "Try what?"

"*Flyyyyyyyyyyy,*" said the Goose Prince. On the moving air the word flowed on and on, not dying away.

Georgie was filled with longing. But she was afraid. She held on, wrapping her fingers together more tightly, shutting her eyes and pressing her cheek against the soft feathers of his neck. Not now. She couldn't do it now. Not yet.

"Just slip off and glide," said the Goose Prince. "You'll see. The wind is just right. It will hold you, if you try it now." And then he warbled it again in his soft fluting voice, *"Flyyyyyyyyyyy."*

For a moment longer Georgie kept her shoulders stiff and her arms pressed close against him. But then she opened her eyes and commanded all her muscles to go limp. Letting go, she slid down the feathery slope of his back until she felt something nudge at her from below. It was a pillow of air, lifting her, holding her steadily and firmly like the palm of a supporting hand. Then at last all the stringy little muscles in Georgie's body loosened. Spreading her arms, she floated on the column of air. Beside her, the Goose Prince floated too, watching her, his hovering wingtips brushing her fingers. Together they drifted, wheeling down and down in slowly descending circles, broad and wide, around and around the pond. Georgie wanted to say, "Oh, look, look at me!" but whenever she opened her mouth, the wind filled it. They were floating, soaring, skimming like sea gulls, like hawks, like swallows. Above them there was nothing but crystal air, and below them—and then for the first time Georgie looked down, and at once she was frightened. The emptiness below her was an immense gulf of nothingness. There was only the steely surface of the gray pond, far down, flat like metal, and the dark bristle of the trees poking up around it. Georgie gave a strangled cry, and dropped one arm.

Instantly she was falling, spinning over and over, plummeting straight down. But only for an instant. With a tremendous jerk and a terrible pinching pain in her left arm, she was snatched out of her plunging fall. The Goose Prince was dragging her through the air, his wings thundering, struggling to hold her aloft. And soon he was lowering her gently to the ground on the nearest shore.

Georgie lay on the stony path for a moment, trying not to cry, and then she stood up, trembling, rubbing her arm. "I'm sorry," she said.

But the Goose Prince was gallant. "Oh, it's *quite* all right," he said. "I hope I didn't hurt you?"

"No, no," said Georgie. "Could we try again?"

"Try again? Are you sure?" The Goose Prince cocked his head at her, and she couldn't help laughing. In his tender concern he looked for a minute more like her mother than like the splendid prince he really was.

"Oh, yes!"

They tried again. Once more the Goose Prince paddled out into the water, once more they took off in a rush of beating wings, once more he lifted Georgie high over the pond. And once again Georgie let go. This time when she clenched her teeth and slid off the back of the Goose Prince, she was careful not to look down. This time she lay perfectly still on the cushion of air. Keeping her arms spread wide, she circled like the Goose Prince as he rested beside her on the same sturdy ridge of warm vapor rising from the pond. She was safe now, perfectly safe. Watching her companion out of the corner of her eye, Georgie obediently copied his slightest motion. Whenever he adjusted the curve of his pinions to change the direction of his flight, Georgie bent her elbows too, and followed his lead. When the wind rocked him, and he spread the tips of his wings to let it flow through the gaps between his feathers, it rocked Georgie too, and she opened her fingers. Glide, glide, float and glide, lift and soar! Oh, how far she could see! All the way to Boston! There it was, the city of Boston, a cluster of dark towers against the sunrise, and there were the shadowy mountains, still blue with night, far away on the other side!

Proudly the Goose Prince flew beside Georgie, wingtip to fingertip, his head bent on his long neck to watch her. The sunlight was shining redly on his belly with the same streaking ray that warmed her own face. And then, at last, Georgie dared to cock her head and look down. She saw Route 2, there at the place where it turned the corner, and, look! there was the train! It was rattling along the shore of the pond on its toy track, shaking from side to side. Now the sun had risen far enough to shine on the trees around the pond. The tops of the trees were pink. For an instant the sun flashed back into Georgie's eyes from the window of a car in the parking lot, making her blink. But she banked and turned, following the lead of the Goose Prince, lifting her head to gaze once again over the whole broad landscape from horizon to horizon, feeling the sleeves of her jacket fill with air, listening to the legs of her pajamas flap like the laundry at home on a breezy day.

She was free. Georgie exulted. At last she was free as air. With the Goose Prince she could fly everywhere, all over the world. There were no fences to keep them out. So this was the way birds felt! They could fly to China and France and Africa! To Africa, where there were lions and elephants! She could fly to the elephants' jungle! She could see monkeys, leaping in the trees!

Sitting in his car in the parking lot at Walden Pond, Ralph Preek gazed up at the giant birds circling in the sky. He was nearsighted. He couldn't see the birds clearly, but he knew that there were two of them, and that one of them was bigger than the other. Idly he picked up the gun that lay beside him on the front seat and pointed it upward, trying to follow the bigger of the two birds with the sights along the barrel. It was just for practice. Of course he wouldn't fire a shot until an instant after midnight on the first morning of the hunting season. But it was too bad to be forced to wait because of a stupid law. Ah, well, the first day of the hunting season was only a little more than two weeks off. He would bide his time. No one would ever be able to say that Ralph Preek was anything but a law-abiding man. Mr. Preek didn't know it, but there was another Massachusetts state law against firing a gun at waterfowl after sundown. And there was still another against the use of firearms at Walden Pond at any time of the day, all year round. Smiling to himself in his ignorance, Mr. Preek put his gun down beside him on the seat of the car, revved the engine softly, and backed the car out of the parking lot.

His time would come. Only two weeks from Saturday. He could wait.

19

TINY SPRINGS AND LITTLE WHEELS

BACK IN HER BED AT home Georgie had hardly closed her eyes before it was time to get up again. But she wasn't tired. She woke up and got dressed and went downstairs even before her mother came to wake her up for school. Flying half the night didn't make Georgie tired. Flying was like resting. Resting on a bed of air.

In the empty kitchen the cornflakes rattled noisily out of the box. Two cats were curled in a patch of slanting morning sunlight. Heat was beginning to collect in the kitchen. It would be a hot day for the middle of September. Three or four flies were droning around the ceiling, hovering, crisscrossing, their buzzes mounting at different harsh pitches. One of the flies landed on the table and walked toward Georgie's bowl of cornflakes. Then it stopped and rubbed its hands together. Georgie put her cheek down on the table and looked at the fly's big eyes. "Hello, there," whispered Georgie. "You know what? You're not the only one who can fly."

"Drat those flies." It was Uncle Freddy, coming into the kitchen in his red bathrobe, reaching for the fly-swatter. "They're coming in from out-of-doors. They know the weather is going to turn cold." Uncle Freddy brandished the flyswatter around the room. Then he saw the fly on the table. "Don't move," he said to Georgie, poising the flyswatter over the fly.

Georgie sat up quickly and clapped her hands.

The fly flew away.

Uncle Freddy gasped and stared after it. Then he laughed, and hung the flyswatter back on its nail on the wall. "Oh, fly, live forever," cried Uncle Freddy. "May your children and grandchildren populate the earth, a hundred thousand strong!"

Georgie's mother came running into the kitchen, her face drawn and pale, her dressing gown buttoned the wrong way. When she saw Georgie, she stopped and sat down hard at the table. Then she reached over quickly and patted Georgie's cheek.

Eddy was next. He came in sleepily, wearing only his

pajama bottoms, opened the bread box, dropped two pieces of bread into the toaster, sat down at the table, and yawned hugely.

Eleanor was last. She strolled into the kitchen with her French book in her hand and plumped herself down at the table. Eleanor was dressed to the teeth for school. Everything was blue. Her skirt was blue. So was her shirt. There were pieces of blue yarn in her red hair. She opened her French book and hung over it, cramming for a test, murmuring French verbs to herself while the TV flickered on the windowsill, muttering its pale green morning news.

Idly Georgie dipped her spoon in the milk at the bottom of her bowl and scooped up a last mouthful of soggy cornflakes. Then she glanced up at her mother and Uncle Freddy and Eddy and Eleanor.

They didn't know. They didn't know she could fly. They could see her cheeks going up and down, they could see the trickle of milk leaking out of one side of her mouth, but they couldn't see what she was thinking. Georgie wiped her mouth and watched Uncle Freddy pour cream into his coffee. The cream swirled in curling patterns in the top of the cup. Uncle Freddy looked back at Georgie and smiled at her—but Uncle Freddy couldn't see the Goose Prince inside her head, floating beside her over Walden Pond, he couldn't see the ground spreading below them to the edge of the world. He could see only the outside of her, not the inside. Of course if she were to pull up her sleeve, then Uncle Freddy would be able to see the black-and-blue mark on her left arm, where the Goose Prince had caught her when she was falling out of the sky—the sore place ached a little, but Georgie didn't rub it. Her arm lay still in her lap.

It was because people had thick smooth outsides like the walls of houses. When you walked past houses in the street, you couldn't see the people inside. And it was like Uncle Freddy's wristwatch. Uncle Freddy had opened it up for Georgie, to show her how it worked. The inside was full of tiny springs and little wheels going back and forth and back and forth. Secretly. Quietly. There inside the watch where nobody could see. Like Eleanor. Just look at Eleanor! Eleanor had her book open on the table, and her hair was orange and her shirt was blue and she was glancing up at Georgie out of the corner of her eye. Eleanor was thinking something secret too, and Georgie didn't know what it was. Inside Eleanor's head the little springs and wheels were going back and forth and back and forth. Quietly. Secretly. Inside where nobody could see.

I wish I knew what's the matter with Georgie, thought Eleanor, looking back down at her French book.

j'aime   *nous aimons*
tu aimes   *vous aimez*
il aime, elle aime *ils aiment*

said the French book. Eleanor turned the French words into English under her breath.

I love   *we love*
you love   *you love*
he loves, she loves *they love*

Something was the matter with Georgie. Oh, whatever would happen to her? What if she grew up a little bit weird and peculiar? That would be terrible! Eleanor stared down at her book, but her attention was drifting away to other kitchens in other parts of the town of Concord. What did Robert Toby eat for breakfast? And Arthur Hathaway?

There was a small explosion. Eddy's toast popped out of the toaster. The two pieces were just right, warm but still soft. Eddy buttered them, then folded one piece over on itself and took a bite out of the middle. The middle bite was always delicious. The middle bite was the best bite. The middle bite was The Bite. Eddy chewed The Bite and looked at Georgie. She was sitting quietly, staring into her empty bowl. Her mouth was open. If you didn't know any better you would think she was a dumb little kid, thought Eddy. But she wasn't. Georgie had learned to read the dictionary when she was only four. Eddy felt a noble impulse of brotherly generosity. "Hey, Georgie," he said, holding out his second slice of toast, "you want a piece?"

Georgie smiled at him and shook her head. Then she hopped out of her chair and squatted down on the floor to pet one of the cats.

"Oh, well, then," said Eddy. He folded the piece of toast over and took The Bite.

Aunt Alex watched Georgie stroke Aphrodite's whiskers and scratch behind her ears. Georgie's mother felt heavy and tired. She didn't know what to think about Georgie. She didn't know what to do. Georgie had flown away twice in the middle of the night. She had come back twice, safe and sound. But what if—?

Aunt Alex held her knife in the air over her soft-boiled egg and stared at the shining blade. What if he came again to take Georgie away? What if he kept on coming? Should she let Georgie go?

Aunt Alex gave Georgie a flashing glance. Then she looked back at her knife and tapped the eggshell firmly. The egg cracked neatly into two parts.

Yes, she should. She would let her go. It was a precious thing. She mustn't be afraid. She wouldn't say a word. Oh, Georgie—Aunt Alex gazed at her daughter and worried silently—what do you see in the air in front of you? Not the cat, not the side of the stove with the drips coming down? What is it, Georgie?

But Georgie was jumping up now and running to the window. *A-WARK, a-WARK!* Another flock of Canada geese was flying over the house. Uncle Freddy got up too and went to the window and stood beside Georgie, gazing upward at the geese, who were flapping in a ragged line through the warm September sky.

Georgie was a little wild thing, too, like the geese, thought Uncle Freddy. She knew something he didn't know. Or something he had forgotten. Something too young and wild for him to remember. Oh, he'd give anything to remember!

The flock had set off from Walden in the direction of Bateman's Pond, but now they began wheeling in a great arc over the town, heading southwest. The young gander who was in the lead was climbing higher and higher in the sky, gabbling noisily, giving directions. Obediently the flock flapped after him, shouting a chorus of frantic questioning and noisy understanding and consent. Soon they all stopped shouting and flew silently together, passing along a wave of air from wing to powerful wing. They were determined. They were earnestly resolved. They were ready to fly all day. This was not to be another short flight from pond to river, from marshy meadow to stubble field. In the minds of the full-grown geese an image of the day's destination was fixed and clear. It was a blue pond farther south, a small body of water surrounded by rocky pastures. And at the end of another day's journey still farther to the south and west they would look for a particular quiet harbor where a long wooden dock stretched out into the water. They would rest there and then fly on, farther and farther to the south. The entire flock of sixty geese was on the move again.

And this morning they were not alone. Other flocks of migrating waterfowl were streaming south over the town of Concord. The whole Atlantic flyway was noisy with ducks and geese. Commuters at the crossing of Walden Street and Route 2 could look up from their cars and see a small nervous family of buffleheads darting overhead. And far away against the vastness of the morning sky another squawking, undulating line was an enormous flock of Canadas from Newfoundland. The great flock of sixty Canada geese that had dallied so long in the mild September air, resting and feeding in Concord's ponds and rivers and fields, was only part of a great movement of other geese, and of brants and mallards and mergansers and blue-winged teal and every other kind of migrating waterfowl, rising from shiny spots of water all along the coast of New England in their hundreds and thousands, to carry on the long journey to their wintering grounds in the south.

Sixty geese? No, sixty minus one. As the flock soared high over Walden Pond, and higher still over Sandy Pond in Lincoln, and higher and higher and higher until the Atlantic Ocean rose in a flat blue line on the horizon to the southeast, the largest bird in the flock dipped one wing and turned in a wide arc and flew back to the water meadows of the Concord River. Silently he dropped to the surface of the river and splashed down, skimming across the choppy water with his wings spread wide, folding them at last and rocking up and down, then paddling slowly to dabble in the shallows in Fair Haven Bay, and duck his head to feed on patches of submerged grass around the island near the western shore.

The Goose Prince was staying on alone.

20

FLEDGLING NO LONGER

*T*HE MOON HAD COME back into the sky. It was growing bigger and bigger. It had been just a sliver at first, a crescent hanging in the evening sky like a fragile ornament just after sunset. But now it was large and lopsided, bigger than half, smaller than full. Night after night the vague shadowy eyes of the moon looked in at Georgie's window, and gazed and gazed at her until she woke up and lifted her head and looked back at it face to face. Then Georgie would lie awake, flat on her back in bed, waiting and waiting. She had taken to going to bed in her clothes. Her overalls and sweater were hot under the covers. She would push back the blankets and lie quietly, expectantly, until the

Goose Prince would tap gently on the window, and then she would hop eagerly out of bed and pull on Eddy's jacket and push up the window softly and climb out.

Night after night the air was crisp and clear. There were no clouds. There was no rain. Night after night Georgie and the Goose Prince flew up and away, over the laundry line, over the garage, over Miss Prawn's plastic garden, over the cabbages, over the high school, over the highway, over the woods. Night after night they glided down at last and splashed on the dark surface of Walden, with the foam rising in sparkling fountains on either side and the moonlight rocking in shattered pieces on the broken mirror of the pond.

And then Georgie would tuck her feet up high, because the water was *cold* now, *freezing cold*, and they would paddle to the shore of Henry's cove, sailing grandly away from the new flock of geese that lay sleeping on the other side of the pond. Often the new geese would wake up to cluck at the intruder who was making a midnight commotion (so *late*, it was *shocking*)—and then they would nestle their sleepy heads down once again in their drowsy feathers and go back to sleep.

The short walk up the hill to the place of the granite posts had become a nightly ritual. Every night Georgie and the Goose Prince climbed the steep slope side by side. Every night, as the moon grew bigger and bigger, and as the leaves of the oak trees parted from their stems one by one and fell to the ground, the splashes of light on the deep rustling floor of the woods grew wider and brighter. And every night the snagged trunks of the pine trees threw out their evergreen arms over the rest of the thin forest. And every half hour the train went racketing along the western shore of the pond in the middle of the night, breaking the quiet of the shadowy woods with its whining rattle and its flashing windows and the dying hum in the rails after it had vanished around the curving track.

Sitting among fallen pine needles and oak leaves, waiting for the Goose Prince to finish his nightly nap, Georgie often listened for the train. And there were other noises, birds murmuring in their sleep, the almost inaudible cracklings and patterings of the small creatures that lived in the underbrush. Waiting patiently, Georgie would listen to everything. Sometimes when the wind was right she could hear the bell of the First Parish Church strike the hour. Most of the time there was no sound at all. In the daytime it was different. In the daytime everything rushed this way and that way, and there was loud talking and yelling, and cars honking and trucks booming along Route 2, and overhead in the sky the sun hurling down bold sheets of yellow. But at night everything just lay still and breathed quietly, as if it were thinking. The moon looked down at everything, but it never made a sound. It kept its secrets. It never told.

Sometimes it was the rattle of the train that woke the Goose Prince from his nap. Georgie would see him start awake, jerking his head up from the soft pillow of his back, and then he would stand and *streeeeeeetch* his wings and open his black beak in a wide comfortable *yaaaaaaaawn*, and preen himself, and then he would waddle over to Georgie, his cheeks bulging in his friendly, beaming smile.

And then would come the time for talking. Not that they ever talked very much. Georgie had never been a great talker, and the Goose Prince himself was a bird of few words. Often instead of talking Georgie would pull something out of the pocket of her denim jacket, some new treasure, and give it to the Goose Prince—another blade of grass for making music or one of the white stones that were Dollabella's puddings. One evening the Goose Prince dipped his bill courteously in an acorn cap and took a sip of air-tea. The next night he stood patiently while Georgie fastened a winged maple seed to his forehead, and then he waddled comically a few steps from side to side, wagging his short tail, to make Georgie laugh. The Goose Prince seemed grateful for everything Georgie brought him. His cheeks would puff out to show his delight. Graciously he would admire it, whatever it was, and then he would tuck it carefully away under a dense pile of leaves beside one of the granite posts.

And then they would fly. It wasn't flying really. It was a kind of elegant slow falling from the very top of the sky. The Goose Prince would carry Georgie high over the pond until it was only a small irregular patch of light far below them, until the world was spread out wide all around and Georgie could see flashing beacons and lighted tankers far out to sea. And then she would slip off and drift downward in long gliding flights, floating on the wind, buoyed by feathery streamers of air.

The air had become Georgie's element. She had taught herself to plunge, to roll and dip and soar. She had caught the knack of a clever assortment of airy acrobatic tricks that were beyond the skill of the Goose Prince himself. Strong as he was, he was heavy in the air, while Georgie was light, only a bit of tossed silk. But of course Georgie couldn't come down on the water by herself. At the bottom of her long slow circling falls she still needed the strong back of the Goose Prince. She would feel him come up beneath her sturdily, until she was settled firmly once again on his back, and then he would carry her up and away, over the trees and over the highway and over the fields and safely home. Every night, as the moon grew bolder . . .

21

RALPH PREEK TRACKS HIS PREY

M R. PREEK WAS DOING research. Research in the field, that was what he called it. He was studying the habits of Canada geese. He had learned to his surprise that the bird he was tracking was not a giant duck after all, but a Canada goose, a single bird, a very large and particular Canada goose. It had become the object of his waking and sleeping dreams.

Sometimes Mr. Preek drove down the dirt road into the Great Meadows beside the Concord River to watch the migrating waterfowl feed in the open marshes. But of course he knew perfectly well that this sort of expedition was a waste of time. The Great Meadows was a wildlife refuge. You couldn't shoot anything there.

Sandy Pond was a better place, Sandy Pond in Lincoln. Mr. Preek often crouched in the woods near the spot where the little island rose out of the water near the shore, and watched the geese take off and land. And sometimes after his working day at the bank was over, late in the afternoon, he would drive to Nine Acre Corner, where he had once seen an enormous flock of geese feeding on a new growth of winter rye in a farmer's field.

A field! A farmer's field! A field would be the very best place for a sharp shot from his new gun to bring the big bird down! A field where the geese were ruining a cash crop, interfering with the livelihood of some good Concord farmer! But the trouble was, Mr. Preek never saw his own very particular Canada goose at Nine Acre Corner, or in the Great Meadows, or around the island in Sandy Pond.

Only at Walden. Like clockwork every night the bird turned up at Walden Pond. It was one of a pair. The other bird was small, but the big one was the largest bird Ralph Preek had ever seen. The two birds came and went every night from the cove on the northern shore of the pond. Watching them night after night from his car in the parking lot, he had worked out a plan. He knew what to do. On the first day of the hunting season he would find himself a blind in the bushes there, a hiding place, and await his chance.

The first day of the hunting season would also be the day of the full moon. That was a piece of luck. Even in the dead of night there would be plenty of light. He would bring down the bird at the full of the moon.

Bring down the bird—Mr. Preek didn't think to himself in words like *killing* and *murder.* He didn't say to himself, *It is all right to kill things.* He simply thought what most hunters think, that nature itself kills things, that hunting is only a part of the balance of nature. If you didn't kill things there would soon be too many things. They would multiply and multiply, and feed on other things, and before long they would overrun the earth. Like locusts! Think of locusts, darkening the sky! Consuming entire counties of growing crops and moving on and gobbling every single leaf in their terrible jaws!

22

ELEANOR HAS A BIRTHDAY

"*I*F SHE DIDN'T GET GOING in five minutes she would be late for school. But it was her birthday, and Eleanor was determined to finish her new dress and wear it in honor of the day. The sewing machine droned *BUZZzzzUZZzzzUZZZ* as Eleanor pressed the button on the floor with her foot. Hunched over the machine, she overstitched the last corner of the neck edging. There. That was it. She was all done. Briskly Eleanor pulled up the lever, leaned forward, bit the threads, and pulled her dress free. She shook it smooth. Then she ran swiftly upstairs to her own room, jerked off her bathrobe, slipped the dress over her head, and twirled in front of the mirror. The dress floated free, then wrapped itself around her legs and floated free again. It was a yellow dress, with a dashing pattern of orange spots and splotches. The splotches matched her orange hair. Eleanor was pleased. She had a new-clothes feeling of happiness. She felt fresh and smart, jaunty and trim, tall and willowy and supple. Snatching up her books, she ran out the door, dodging Uncle Freddy's students, who were coming up the walk. With her hair flying and her skirt flowing out behind her, Eleanor plunged romantically past an admiring Arthur Hathaway. Arthur turned around and whistled.

Aunt Alex had plans for Eleanor's birthday too, but in the middle of her last afternoon class she suddenly sniffed the air, rushed for the kitchen, jerked the cake pans out of the oven, and dropped them *bang, bang* on the drainboard of the sink. It was a little too late. The two layers were dry and thin and black on the bottom. But an hour later Eleanor's birthday cake was a triumph, a spectacular example of the art of the amateur cake decorator. Aunt Alex had whipped up three batches of lumpy frosting, and then she had lathered the two lopsided layers with the white batch, and now Eddy and Georgie were squirting frosting decorations all over the outside with the yellow batch and the green batch.

Georgie used the little flat-nosed nozzle on the pastry tube to make clusters of green leaves on the top of the cake (you push and squeeze, then flick the nozzle up). Eddy draped yellow swags around the side with the fancy little star-shaped gadget (you have to keep moving and squeezing, both at the same time). Aunt Alex had manufactured a dozen globby roses the night before on little squares of wax paper. Now she took them out of the refrigerator and slid one of them on a cluster of Georgie's leaves.

"Oh, no," said Aunt Alex, stepping back to look. "It won't do. It's too much."

"No, it's not," said Eddy. "You can't have too much frosting on a cake."

"It reminds me of Miss Prawn's front yard," said Aunt Alex. Reluctantly she stuck the rest of her vulgar roses all over the rim of the cake.

Then Georgie screwed a new nozzle on her pastry tube, knelt on the kitchen stool, gripped her sides tightly with her elbows, sucked in her lower lip, and wrote *Eleanor* across the middle of the cake in a flowing hand.

The front door slammed. Georgie paused with her pastry tube in the air. Eddy stopped running his finger around the bowl of green frosting. Aunt Alex looked up from the blackened cake pans in the sink. Exposed in plain sight on the table was Eleanor's birthday cake, gorgeous with thick smudgy frosting, encrusted with shapeless roses and sprawling leaves, heavy with drooping swags, crowned with Eleanor's name in yellow sugar.

Eleanor burst into the kitchen. She threw open the door and stood staring at the three of them. "A giraffe," shouted Eleanor. "My dress, it makes me look like a giraffe."

They gaped at her.

"My dress. It's Robert Toby. He says I look like a giraffe. He does. That's what he says." Eleanor's eyes were glittering. Her hair was wild, all tumbled to one side.

"Oh, well." Aunt Alex dismissed Robert Toby with a wave of her hand. "He just likes to tease you, isn't that it?"

"*Oh*, no, he doesn't." Eleanor slapped her books down on the table. The cake bounced. "Not Robert Toby. He's so *sincere*. I mean, he *really* says what he really *thinks*. He says I look like a— And after I slaved! You saw me slave! Didn't I slave, Aunt Alex? I wore my fingers to the bone! Eleven *buttonholes*." Eleanor stared vaguely at the cake. She clawed at her hair. "I'll never wear this dress again. I'll die before I'll wear it again!"

"He's crazy, that Robert Toby," said Eddy slyly. "You don't look like a giraffe. Why would anybody say that? You look like an ostrich. A sick ostrich with the chicken pox."

Eleanor shrieked and threw herself at her little

brother and slapped him twice.

Aunt Alex opened her mouth to say, *Stop it at once*, then thought better of it. Eddy was shouting. Eleanor whirled out of the room, tearing at her new dress, ripping at the buttons in the buttonholes. Buttons popped off and bounced on the floor. She slammed the kitchen door. Then Eddy whammed the door open again, *crash* against the wall, and yelled after her, "Some people just can't stand the truth about themselves, that's all that's the matter with them." Then Eddy stamped out too and slammed the door. There was an awful *screeeeeeech* from one of the cats. "Oh, sorry," said Eddy. He picked up the cat and slammed the door again with a final *crash*.

Aunt Alex and Georgie were left alone in the kitchen. The silence throbbed.

Georgie didn't understand what was the matter with Eleanor. Her dress was pretty! Sort of spotted and pretty and bright yellow. The spots were like the spots on an animal's back, like the spots on the cats, or the dog down the street—or a giraffe! Really pretty.

Aunt Alex sighed. Reaching down with one long arm, she picked up a button from the floor. Georgie got down on hands and knees, poked her narrow hand under the refrigerator and brought out another.

"Thank you, Georgie dear." Georgie's mother put the

buttons in her apron pocket and looked helplessly at the cake. The top layer had slid a little sideways. She nudged it back in place. Silently she handed Georgie one of the bowls of leftover frosting and a spoon. Georgie scraped frosting from the bowl and sucked the spoon. Aunt Alex began cleaning up the sticky table.

How different they are, thought Aunt Alex, Eleanor and Georgie. Altogether different. And it isn't just that Georgie is younger. Georgie is different from Eleanor all the way through, from the inside out. Why, look at her, right now. She doesn't even know that she exists. She's just eyes and ears, that's all she is, just looking and listening. She doesn't think about herself at all. The world outside her rushes into her, and that's what she becomes. She doesn't think to herself, "This is me, Georgie." Instead she pulses with the sunrise and the rain and the geese flying over the house. She's in them, not outside them. She's more like a bird or a flower than a girl named Georgie. Whereas, Eleanor! Oh, Eleanor! Just look at Eleanor! Eleanor is all Eleanor! And everything outside Eleanor becomes Eleanor too—sisters, brothers, uncles, aunts! She sucks us all in! There isn't anything else but Eleanor in all the world!

The kitchen door opened. It was Eleanor. She had changed her clothes. She was wearing a pair of blue jeans and a shirt with a large red slice of watermelon printed on the front. Her hair poured hotly over her shoulders. Her face was red from crying. "My cake," moaned Eleanor. "Just look at my cake. It's beautiful, really beautiful. Oh, Aunt Alex, I'm sorry."

Eleanor collapsed against Aunt Alex and howled.

23

MISS PRAWN LEANS
IN AGAIN

*E*LEANOR'S BIRTHDAY was the same day as the full
moon. Eleanor didn't notice that the moon was
full. Georgie did. So did Miss Prawn.

And therefore Miss Prawn was leaning in again,
secretly, pressing against the people in the neighboring
house as she had so often done before, making a new
claim. It wasn't because she liked them. Oh, no! No,
indeed! In fact, Miss Prawn found nothing but fault with
all of them, all five of them, big and small. And yet somehow she couldn't leave them alone. She had even moved
herself into the house next door, bag and baggage, just
so that she could be even more outraged by the tomfool
things they could be trusted to keep right on doing. It

was horrifying and fascinating, somehow, just to see what those people would think of next.

Uncle Freddy couldn't understand it. What did the woman want? Why did she go right on poking in her nose? Aunt Alex knew why. One day when Uncle Freddy was protesting a new Prawnish assault, yet another rap on the glass, some further pressure from next door, Aunt Alex had explained it to him fiercely. "It's your *goodness* that attracts her, that's what it is. She can't stand it. She has to poke it and prod it and pinch it and squeeze it and try as hard as she can to squash it entirely. Only she can't. And it drives her mad."

Eleanor's birthday cake was delicious. There was so much frosting on the outside, nobody paid any attention to the compacted dryness of the inside.

After the cake came the presents. One present was a lamp from Eddy and Georgie. Eddy had made it at school. It was a pump lamp, like an old-fashioned pump in the backyard. When you pumped the handle, the light turned on. Georgie had bought a lampshade in the dime store and decorated it with red maple leaves. She had ironed the leaves between pieces of waxed paper and stuck them on the shade.

Eleanor unwrapped the lamp and squealed with delight. Eddy plugged it in. The light shone through the red leaves. "Wow," cried Eleanor, "just look at those leaves." Georgie giggled with pleasure. Then Eleanor opened the rest of her presents, and there were more rapturous squeals and ecstatic screams. The kitchen was loud with Eleanor's noise.

Suddenly Georgie felt hot. She had eaten too much cake. She said, "Excuse me," and slipped out of the kitchen. In the front hall the lady on the newel post towered over her. The lady's lamp was turned off, because the sky outside had only just turned dark, but moonlight slanted through the oval window in the front door and spread a thin ray over the marble ear of Henry Thoreau.

Georgie looked at Henry's ear. She wanted to whisper in it, to tell Henry about the pond and the flocks of geese on the water, and the Goose Prince, and flying, and how nice it was at Walden in the middle of the night, did he remember? But then she was attracted by the brilliant moonlight on the knobby pillars and crisscross lattice of the front porch, and she went outdoors.

The porch was cool, dazzling with the splendor of the full moon, which was rising pale and calm over the Mill Brook meadow. The moon looked as big and round as the porch light.

Georgie leaned against the railing and stared at the moon. Why did it come up later every night? She thought about it and felt her fat stomach. The moon was heavier, that was it. It got rounder and rounder every night, and heavier and heavier, and so it came up slower and slower.

There were bubbles of paint on the porch railing. In the moonlight Georgie could see them clearly. She dented one with her finger. Then she took hold of one of the pillars and pulled herself up until she was standing on the railing with one arm twined around the pillar. Dreamily she stared over the meadow at the moon. Then she let go of the pillar, spread her arms wide, and bent her knees, intending to spring lazily over the bushes and drift down into the front yard.

"STOP."

Something was rising out of the bushes with a shriek.

Georgie squealed, and her easy jump collapsed in midair. She fell. A stiff broken wand of hydrangea raked her side.

It was Madeline Prawn, standing up skinny and tall in the middle of the bushes. "Oh, no, you don't," gasped Miss Prawn, "not this time." Jerking Georgie to her feet, she clung to her and thrashed about in the bushes, confused by the brilliant contrasts of light and shade. At last she crashed her way out of the bushy tangle and dragged Georgie up on the porch and barged into the dark front hall and fumbled for the light switch, hallooing for Frederick and Alexandra Hall.

Everyone came running. "I warned you," cried Miss Prawn, staring around in savage triumph at the circle of shocked faces, "I warned you about the full moon. The child was taking off. She was flying away. She was going home to the fairies. Didn't I tell you to watch out? You can't say I didn't warn you!"

"Merciful heavens," said Uncle Freddy, "my dear Miss Prawn, whatever do you mean? Let go of the child at once!"

But Miss Prawn hung on. The more Georgie squirmed, the tighter was Miss Prawn's grip. The time had come for the Georgie Protection Society to spring into action. With one accord Eddy and Eleanor flung themselves on Madeline Prawn.

It was three against one. Four feverish bodies wrestled in the dark, while Uncle Freddy and Aunt Alex stood on the sidelines, dazed and shaken by the vibration, knocked against by tussling arms and legs. Georgie yanked and struggled, trying to jerk herself free, Eddy clutched Georgie around the waist, trying to drag her away, Eleanor wrenched at Miss Prawn's two hands, prying up her fingers one at a time, and Miss Prawn kicked out blindly and uttered muffled cries. At last Eleanor sank her teeth into Miss Prawn's thumb. (It wasn't the first time. Miss Prawn had felt the imprint of

140

Eleanor's teeth before.) Now she shrieked and let go of Georgie. Georgie ran to her mother, and Eddy and Eleanor backed away, breathing hard.

It was all over. Aunt Alex stared at Miss Prawn, her eyes blazing. (Aunt Alex didn't get angry very often.) "Just what *is* it you are trying to say, Miss Prawn?"

"The moon," said Miss Prawn again, panting, rubbing her shin where Eddy had kicked it, sucking her thumb. "I've told you and told you. Don't you remember what I said?" She closed her eyes and groaned. "Oh, why do I care what happens to the lot of you? Why, oh, why, should I be my brother's keeper? Why should I bother with my neighbor's welfare? But it's just the way I was born. I can't help it. A natural-born instinct for doing good and helping others. Now listen. It's a time of danger, the full of the moon. Disaster. I mean, it's a well-known scientific fact."

The five of them were staring back at her, Frederick and Alexandra Hall and their three impossible children. No, there were six, counting the metal woman on the staircase. No, seven! There were seven! The seventh was the grim stony visage of the bust of Henry Thoreau. Seven pairs of eyes were boring into Miss Prawn. Hatefully. Accusingly. Ungratefully.

Miss Prawn's lip trembled. She was only trying to help. To do her duty as a neighbor and friend. After all, it was *she* who had been vouchsafed . . . After all, far be it from *her* . . . Oh, it wasn't fair. It just wasn't fair at all!

Uncle Freddy felt sorry for Miss Prawn. He took charge. With perfect courtesy he began pouring oil on troubled waters. Stepping forward, he took her by the arm. "On the contrary, my dear Miss Prawn, in my opinion the monthly appearance of the full moon is a time of great good fortune." Smoothly he guided her out onto the porch and down the steps to the front walk. "You have only to study the nocturnal wanderings of our good Henry Thoreau, Miss Prawn, during the summer of 1851. Have you ever happened to glance at his journal for that year? Oh, you should! You really should!" They were out the front gate. They were gliding along the sidewalk and up the path to Miss Prawn's house. "I'm sure, Miss Prawn, you too would find it a record of blessing and joy." Uncle Freddy deposited Miss Prawn on her own front stoop. "What a glorious history it is, indeed, of the passage of the full summer moon over the rivers and fields of the town of Concord! Good night, my dear Miss Prawn!"

Miss Prawn was dizzy. For a moment she hardly knew where she was. But then, as Uncle Freddy ran up the steps of the porch next door, she took a deep breath and recovered some of her senses. Turning to the vague dark shape of the neighboring house with its porches swimming in moonlight, she called out, "Keep an eye on her! Don't say I didn't warn you!"

Aunt Alex opened the door for Uncle Freddy and watched him lean over the porch railing and toss a final salute to Miss Prawn. "It's very kind of you, Madeline, but I assure you, we can look after Georgie ourselves."

But can we? worried Aunt Alex in the middle of the night, lying wide awake beside a sleeping Uncle Freddy, listening to the rushing beat of the great wings and the quiet scrape of Georgie's window sliding upward. Filled with dread, she sat up and caught a last glimpse of Georgie clinging to the goose's back, lifting from the porch, vanishing into the night. Would she come back? Of course she would, of course, of course. She had come back many times before. There was really no need to worry.

The room was chill. Aunt Alex shivered and lay down again and stared up at the dark ceiling. Beside her, Uncle Freddy had turned over on his back. He was snoring gently. But Uncle Freddy's snoring wasn't the sort of noise that would break the silence, the kind of silence that muffled Aunt Alex now, a silence that fell like motes of dust around her from every side of the shadowy room, that drifted over her like blowing snow, piling its nothingness around her, covering her over, burying her, mounding above her in soft layers to the ceiling.

There was only one sound in the world that could cut through that mortal stillness: the sound of Georgie coming back, the scrabbling noise of the great webbed feet on the porch roof, the scraping of the window in its frame, the light spring of the bed in the next room.

Aunt Alex lay in bed with her jaw tightly set and her fingers clenched, while the silence weighed down on her face. How much longer could she bear it?

24

MR. PREEK TAKES
DEADLY AIM

"*A-WARK, A-WARK!*" The Goose Prince skimmed low above the surface of the pond where the reflection of the moon lay in a broad column of moving light. Far away on the other side Georgie could see heads jerking up among the sleeping flock, and here and there a scandalized flapping of wings. A mild scolding crackle drifted across the water. Then the spray dashed up around her and the moonlight broke into a thousand pieces. The water wallowed and slopped. Then it smoothed, and the moon was again a single rippling column. Serenely, with the bluff prow of his breast parting the water, hardly disturbing the liquid surface at all, the Goose Prince sailed to the shore of Henry's cove.

On the steep slope to the clearing in the woods the moon shone bald and bright through the open branches of the trees. Georgie walked up the hill beside the Goose Prince with her hand resting lightly on his back. Then she settled down on the leafy floor of the clearing while he took his nap. When he woke up, she took a fresh blade of grass out of her pocket and played him a tune. It was only a succession of hoarse breathy notes, but they vibrated on the still air with a haunting excitement like that of his own hooting cry, and she could see that the Goose Prince was pleased. With his usual regal courtesy he picked up Georgie's blade of grass in his beak and tucked it carefully under his pile of leaves. "Shall we go for a spin?" he said politely, bending his neck forward in the kindly gesture Georgie knew so well.

"Oh, yes, of course." Impulsively, without meaning to, without thinking about it at all, Georgie put her arms around his neck, kissed him smartly on the end of his beak, and stepped back, smiling.

The Goose Prince didn't turn into a man. He merely stood there, beaming at Georgie, his cheeks bulging in the funny way that meant he was smiling too. And then, not saying anything, because they never really needed to say anything to each other, they walked side by side, true friends and loving companions, down to the shore of the pond.

A moment later they were side by side in common possession of the air, drenched in moonlight, gliding in lofty circles over the pond.

Georgie saw the car in the parking lot. For an instant the moon glanced into her eye from the slanting windshield. But she barely noticed it. The car had been parked there many times before.

It was only when the smooth billows of creamy air had carried her around and around over the pond and down and down, closer and closer to the water—it was only when the Goose Prince had dropped below her, ready to lift her up at last and carry her home—it was only then that Georgie saw anything out of the ordinary.

The wind had freshened from the north. *Bong, bong, bong*—the midnight bell in the steeple of the First Parish Church was ringing clearly over the water. On the last stroke Georgie caught a glimpse of something glittering in the bushes along the shore. There was a metallic gleam on a long straight shaft. Something blue and shining was lifting, following the dropping arc of the Goose Prince.

Instantly Georgie woke up from her floating suspended dream. In one brilliant flash of understanding she knew what was happening. She knew what to do. Violently Georgie hurled herself downward, plunging between the Goose Prince and the puff of white smoke,

147

shielding him from the great exploding noise that shattered all the world.

Down she fell, straight down into the shallows, while a thousand birds rose together from the other side of the pond, shouting, *DANGER, DANGER, DANGER.*

The warning was too late. With a despairing cry, the Goose Prince plummeted after Georgie, grasped her jacket in his bill, and dragged her out of the water and up on the shore. Then, swollen to twice his size, he made a rush at the clumsy man who was blundering out of the underbrush.

Georgie saw the furious assault. Sitting up and holding her bleeding arm, she watched the Goose Prince stretch out his long neck and throw himself at his enemy, his beak open wide in a terrifying HHHHHHHIIII-IIIIIIISSSSSSSSSSSSSSSSSSSSSSSSS, his thundering wings beating like the plunging hooves of a rearing horse.

The startled man dropped his gun, threw up his arms to protect his face, turned, stumbled away in the direction of the road, fell over a log, struggled to his feet, and staggered forward, beating frantically through the bushes, until suddenly he found himself submerged up to his waist, cursing, in the cold slime of a swampy backwater.

And there the Goose Prince abandoned him. Turning away, he flew swiftly back to Georgie, hooting his dismay and grief.

But Georgie was already helping herself. "I think I'm all right," she said feebly. She had pulled up handfuls of leaves and pine needles. She was stuffing them into her sleeve to soak up the blood that was seeping from the upper part of her arm.

Trembling, the Goose Prince stooped low beside her. "Can you climb on?" he said. Reaching out with her good arm, Georgie struggled weakly up on his back and drooped her head into the hollow place between feathery wing and neck. Then she wrapped her good arm around his breast and gripped the wrist of the other with her good hand.

"Are you all right now?" said the Goose Prince, looking back at her, his great eye at once both fierce and sad. "Can you hold on?"

"Oh, yes," whispered Georgie. "I'm all right. Really I am."

Desperately the Goose Prince ran forward, headlong, trampling the hard-beaten dirt of the path and springing into the air, lifting his precious freight straight up over the trees, bearing her steadily home. Low over the highway, low over the high school, low over the cabbage fields he carried her, until they were circling at last directly over the house with the domed tower and the high peaked roof. This time the Goose Prince sank gently to the window that was next to Georgie's. Then he rattled frantically against the glass with his bill and beat against it with his wings, hooting, "*A-WARK, a-WARK!*"

In an instant the window was thrown open, and Georgie was tumbling through it into her mother's arms. And Uncle Freddy was leaping out of bed, his hair in a frowze. Together Aunt Alex and Uncle Freddy lowered Georgie to the warm bed, and Uncle Freddy pulled up the blankets around her and Aunt Alex ran to the phone to call the doctor.

Only Georgie, lying on the bed with her head lifted up from the pillow, only Georgie saw the Goose Prince peer in at her anxiously, his head craned to one side. Only Georgie saw him fly up from the porch, a heaving black shape, blurred at the edges against the sky. Only Georgie saw the blank window after he was gone. Beyond it the lavish moonlight had washed the sky clear of stars. There was only the window itself, its rectilinear moldings raked by the light of the round moon, which stood now at the very zenith of the heavens, broad and majestic and wide and altogether full. There was only the window and the tremulous disordered curtain, caught between upper sash and lower, bellying out and flapping like the sail of an abandoned vessel.

"Good-bye, good-bye," whispered Georgie, bursting into feeble tears.

25

THE HUMILIATION OF MR. PREEK

RALPH PREEK WAS FURIOUS, humiliated, disappointed. He had failed. He had shot down a Canada goose, but it had been only the smaller of the two, and an odd sort of bird—silhouetted against the moonlight, it had looked distinctly queer. What was worse, he had failed to bag his catch and bring it home. And, worst of all, instead of destroying the bird that was a menace to hearth and home and to the safety of little children, he himself had almost been killed by the bird instead!

Mr. Preek stayed home from the bank and nursed his wounds and sulked. There were savage bites on his arms, on the back of his neck, on his back. The bird was a killer. This time there was no mistake.

But for some reason Mr. Preek's grudge had become entirely personal. He didn't want to bring anyone else into it. He would look so ridiculous—that was the trouble—getting beaten up by a stupid bird!

"It was dogs," he said, lying naked on the doctor's examining table, wincing as the doctor dabbed at him with disinfectant. "Savage dogs. They've been tearing up my flower bed. I was only trying to chase them away, and then look what they did, they attacked me."

"Funny sort of dogs," mused the doctor. "It looks more like somebody came at you with a can opener or a corkscrew." The doctor chuckled. "Are you sure it wasn't just a barroom brawl?"

"Oh, no, of course not. Don't be absurd. It was dogs, huge beasts with enormous, foaming jaws and colossal teeth and eyes like dinner plates. It's a mercy I got away alive. Oh, ow!"

"Foaming jaws? Were they really foaming at the mouth? Say, you'd better report those animals to the police. Look here, I'm going to have to start you on rabies shots, just in case."

"Shots?" said Ralph Preek. "No, no, I was mistaken. They weren't foaming at the mouth, after all. No, no."

"Well, we better be absolutely sure. Turn over." The doctor dabbed more disinfectant on a shrinking part of Mr. Preek, poised his needle mercilessly over it, and stabbed.

26

AUNT ALEX TAKES
NO CHANCES

*T*HE GEORGIE PROTECTION SOCIETY had failed too.

"I'll bet it was that man in the store. Mr. Preek. That guy in the bank." Eddy pounded his fist on the kitchen table. "It was him, wasn't it, Georgie? The man with the gun? You know, the one who brought you home the other day?"

Georgie was sitting at the table, her arm in a sling, opening her mouth like an infant bird while Eleanor fed her spoonfuls of cornflakes. She swallowed a mouthful and shook her head at Eddy to say she didn't know.

Eleanor was envious. "Gee, Georgie," she said, dipping up another spoonful, "I wish a big goose would take me flying in the sky at night. Was it really wonderful?" In the back of Eleanor's head there was a dim memory of times when she too had been swept up into the air, dreamlike times that had been called into being by the diamond in the window of the little room in the attic, or the swing in the vanished summerhouse, or the stereoscope under Eddy's bed, times when they had been summoned by the handsome woman on the staircase, or by Prince Krishna, their uncle who lived in India. There had been all sorts of adventures, and some of them had been high-flying and far away, hadn't they, high and very far? But she had never flown by herself, had she? She had never been as lucky as that? Or had she? It was all beginning to run together in the back of Eleanor's mind, and the things that had probably really happened were confused with the things that probably hadn't. And every day everything in her whole past life—the real things and the imaginary things—was being pushed farther and farther back, because going to high school was so enormous, so vast! so different from all of Eleanor's life before. The milling crowds in the hall between classes, all those jostling elbows and swollen shoulders and bosoms, all those enormous hands and feet, they pushed and thumped and shoved at Eleanor's childhood, until there was no room anymore for anything but *now*, right *now*, a hurrying rushing *now* that was *just incredibly thrilling* or *absolutely rotten and just disgusting*, this heaving present moment, right *now*.

Georgie looked back at Eleanor and sucked the spoon. Had it been wonderful, Eleanor wanted to know, flying with the Goose Prince? Oh, how could she tell it? Georgie didn't know what to say. She wiped her mouth silently and shook her head at the next spoonful.

"Well, okay, Georgie. No more, then? Well, okay." Briskly Eleanor put down the bowl of cornflakes and bounded out of her chair and snatched up her coat and books and hoisted the strap of her pocketbook over her shoulder and ran out the front door, hurrying away to school.

Within a week Georgie was feeding herself. She was mending quickly. The wound had healed. The pellets had missed the biggest blood vessels in her arm. They had missed the bone. There was only a bandage now, held on with adhesive tape, to show that anything had happened at all. Georgie, too, could go back to school.

But not alone. Aunt Alex had decreed that Georgie was never to be left alone again. Aunt Alex was taking no more chances with a kidnapping Canada goose, no matter how good his intentions, no matter how noble a bird he might be, and gentle and splendid and kind.

And therefore the Georgie Protection Society was back at work, keeping her under guard. Eddy was to walk her to school in the morning and back again in the afternoon. Eleanor was to keep her company at home when Aunt Alex was out shopping or whenever she was busy with a class.

Miss Prawn had been right about Georgie. That was the trouble. In some terrible mistaken interfering way, she had been right after all. And therefore Aunt Alex and Uncle Freddy and the Georgie Protection Society were working full time, taking Miss Prawn's advice at last.

The first thing was the moving of Georgie's bed. Eddy and Uncle Freddy took it apart and carried it across the hall and jammed it into the space between Eleanor's dresser and her desk. Georgie's bed was right under Eleanor's window, but that was all right. There was no porch roof below Eleanor's window. The window looked out over the other side of the yard into Miss Prawn's garden with its tiresome message in plastic flowers. The message was still plain. It still said *WELCOME TO CONCORD*. The white plastic petals of the roses never faded. The green plastic leaves never withered and fell.

"I'm sorry about the view, Georgie," said Eleanor, making the bed for Georgie, tucking in the tufted bedspread.

"Oh, that's all right," said Georgie. She smoothed the spread over the pillow, then turned her head and listened. There was a *bang-bang*ing noise across the hall. "What's Uncle Freddy doing?"

Eleanor avoided Georgie's eyes. "I don't know. Hey, Georgie, where's Dollabella? Oh, there she is. Let's put Dollabella on your pillow. There you go, Dollabella, old girl. Now, see, Georgie? Doesn't she look nice?"

But Georgie wasn't listening. She was walking stiff-legged across the hall. In her old bedroom she found Uncle Freddy hammering nails into the window frame. When Georgie came in, he stopped hammering and looked at her guiltily. "I'm just nailing the window shut to keep it tight until spring comes again. Your room is a little drafty, you see, Georgie."

Georgie nodded silently, and stood watching him, clasping her upper lip with her teeth, rocking back and forth on her heels.

Uncle Freddy hammered in another nail. Then he put the hammer down and turned around. "No, no, it isn't drafty in here at all." Picking up the hammer, he pounded in another nail with a great shivering of the window frame and rattling of the glass. Then he looked at Georgie helplessly and shook his head.

"It's okay," said Georgie. "No, really, I don't mind." And it was okay. It didn't matter. Because it was true— the Goose Prince really mustn't come again. Not now. It was too dangerous. He mustn't come until the end of the month. Georgie had found out about the hunting season. She had asked Eddy, and Eddy had asked Oliver Winslow.

Oliver had a gun. Oliver even had a hunting license. He liked to pop away at bottles and tin cans and squirrels and passing birds and any other innocent thing that dove in front of him across his line of sight. So Oliver knew about the hunting season. He told Eddy, and Eddy told Georgie. The season would be over in less than three weeks. Until then the Goose Prince must stay away. He must hide. Because they were after him! It wasn't just that big fat man with the red face. It was all those other men. There were lots of them. They all had guns. They were everywhere! They were shooting everywhere!

Eleanor woke up suddenly and sat up in bed. Georgie was screaming.

"Georgie, Georgie, stop it." Eleanor jumped out of bed and crossed the room and shook Georgie. The room was gray with feeble dawn light. "You're just having a nightmare. It's all right."

Georgie stopped screaming. She sat bolt upright and stared out the window. "Listen," said Georgie. "I heard something."

Eleanor lifted her head and listened. There was a faint cracking sound far away out-of-doors.

"Don't you hear it?" Georgie grasped Eleanor's wrist. "It's guns. They're shooting over there somewhere."

"Guns?" The cracking sound came again. "Oh, is that

what it is?" said Eleanor. "Well, maybe you're right. But the geese have all flown south, I'll bet." She patted Georgie's hunched shoulder. Georgie's arms were rigid in their sockets. "Your goose has gone away," soothed Eleanor. "You know that."

"But they shouldn't do it," said Georgie. "Those hunters. They shouldn't. They shouldn't."

Then Georgie lay down and allowed herself to be tucked in again, and Eleanor slipped back under her own covers and lay down on her side facing the wall. Poor old Georgie. She took things so hard. All she could think about was that big goose. She needed something to take her mind off her troubles. She needed friends to play with, that was it. If Georgie just had somebody to play with, she wouldn't brood about things so much.

Eleanor closed her eyes and vowed to do something about it. She would find a playmate for Georgie, right away, this very morning before school. She would call up Dorothea Broom before school.

Across the narrow bedroom Georgie lay on her back with her small bones straight and flat under the covers, her stringy sinews pulled up tense and tight, her eyes wide open, staring at the ceiling, listening to the *crackety-crack* of the guns in the faraway woods.

A PLAYMATE FOR GEORGIE

WALKING GEORGIE HOME from school on Monday
afternoon was like dragging a ball and chain.
She kept hanging back. Eddy had to keep
turning around and egging her on. "Come *on*, Georgie."

Home at last, climbing the steps to the front porch,
Eddy breathed a sigh of relief. His guard duty was over.
Georgie was idling through the front gate. A moment
later Eddy was upstairs in his own room looking at the
complicated control-room section of his rocket model.
Pieces were spread out all over his desk. He was ready
to get to work.

Georgie was alone outdoors.

Slowly she climbed the three steps of the front

porch. Then she turned around to look back at the front yard.

There had been a frost in the night. The marigolds along the fence had turned black. Georgie shivered in her puffy winter jacket. The jacket was last year's, too small for her now. Her bare wrists hung out of the sleeves. She held her arms out in front of her and looked at them. Then she bent her knees to jump down over the three steps to the walk below.

Something stopped her. Georgie hesitated and dropped her arms. The air over the wooden steps looked thinned out by the cold, too thin to hold her up, too thin to let her drift down lightly the way she had done before. Georgie decided not to jump after all. She turned away and opened the front door and stepped into the front hall.

Her mother was running toward the door, her face pale in the pitch darkness of the front hall. She was calling something to Eddy. ". . . not to be left alone!"

"It's okay," said Georgie. "Here I am."

Aunt Alex stopped and pressed her hand on her blouse. "Oh, there you are, Georgie dear. My goodness." Then she kissed Georgie lightly, followed her into the kitchen, and watched her hang up her jacket by the back door.

Eleanor was beating eggs in a bowl, whirring the

electric mixer at top speed. Looking up, Eleanor exchanged a flick of a glance with Aunt Alex. Then she turned off the mixer. "Oh, say, Georgie, don't you think you should run upstairs and change your clothes? Dorothea's coming over. Dorothea Broom."

"She *is*?" Georgie was flabbergasted. "Dorothea *Broom*? She's coming over? Right *now*?"

"For tea, you see, Georgie," said Eleanor quickly, scooping up the eggshells and dumping them into the sink. "We just thought it would be nice for you to have a friend over."

Aunt Alex put on an apron. She felt heavy-footed and blundering. "Her mother is coming too," said Aunt Alex. "They're both coming. Oh, Eleanor, we haven't got a lemon. You're supposed to have a lemon, all cut up into slices, very thin."

Georgie was still staring at Eleanor, her mouth open in horror. But Eleanor was slapping down cookie tins. "Here, Georgie," she said recklessly, "hand me that flour sifter, will you? And you really ought to go up and change your clothes. Those good old red overalls of yours are way too small for you now. Look, they're halfway up your legs."

Georgie looked down at herself in dismay. Then she stumped reluctantly upstairs after Eleanor and stood stock-still while Eleanor held bits and pieces of her own clothes up against her, and pulled open drawers, and poked in her closet.

"Here's a funny one, Georgie. My watermelon shirt. It shrank in the wash. I bet it would fit you just right. See? It's only a little bit too big."

Georgie put on the watermelon shirt. She put on an old skirt of Eleanor's. The skirt drooped and sagged. "You're certainly not getting any fatter," said Eleanor. "Just taller. Here, we'll cinch it in around the waist with a belt."

Georgie looked at herself in the mirror while Eleanor pushed and pulled at her and beamed at her over her shoulder. "I think I look like celery," mumbled Georgie.

"Celery?" said Eleanor. "You mean watermelon."

"No, celery," said Georgie. She meant she was long and stringy and thin like a piece of celery. In the mirror her arms hung out of the shirt, blue-white and dangling. Her hair and face were pale like blanched celery.

"Oh, celery," said Eleanor. "Oh, I see what you mean. Well, so do I. We're a couple of long skinny pieces of celery."

Dorothea Broom, on the other hand, was a choice piece of fruit, a succulent peach or a plump grape or a ripe cherry. Dorothea leaned back against her mother's knees in the parlor, while Georgie slumped round-shouldered in a chair on the other side of the room with her feet flat on the floor. (Georgie's feet had never touched the floor in that chair before.)

Mrs. Broom was smiling proudly, patting Dorothea's hair, winding curls around her finger, smoothing Dorothea's dress.

Eleanor gazed at Dorothea.

So did Aunt Alex.

Dorothea's pleased face collected all their looks. Her chubby cheeks absorbed them. She smiled her rosy smile.

Only Georgie didn't look at Dorothea. Georgie looked vaguely at the air in front of her. Driven into a corner in the same room with Dorothea, Georgie looked spindly and pale.

Dorothea had brought her doll. It was a big pink plastic doll with fluffy hair. Its mouth was open in a cooing *O*. "Show Georgina how your doll works, Dorothea," said Mrs. Broom.

Dorothea put her doll on the floor. The doll walked a few stiff steps, then toppled over. Dorothea picked it up. "Listen to this," she said. She pulled a string in the doll's back.

"My name is Bubbles!" said the doll. "I blow bubbles! I love you!"

"She blows bubbles?" said Eleanor. "Does she really?"

"Yes," said Dorothea. "Of course you have to put a bubble pack inside."

"Say, Georgie," said Eleanor, "why don't you go upstairs and get one of your dolls too? You know, show Dorothea."

Georgie's wan face brightened. She ran out of the room and came back a moment later with Dollabella.

"Oh, no, not that one, Georgie," said Eleanor, clapping her forehead. But then she laughed. She laughed too hard. She gasped, "I'll get the cookies," and sprang out of her chair.

Aunt Alex stuck up for Dollabella. "Actually, Georgie," she said loyally, "I like Dollabella best myself."

Dorothea was shocked. She stared at Dollabella. "Is that a doll?"

Mrs. Broom explained. "Oh, Dorothea, it's a terribly *interesting* kind of doll. Made out of a corncob, I think." Mrs. Broom lifted Dorothea into her lap. "Perhaps, Dorothea, someday soon you might give Georgina one of your older dolls to play with. Wouldn't that be a nice thing to do for your new friend?"

Aunt Alex looked out the window and mumbled something under her breath.

Georgie shook her head and hugged Dollabella to her chest.

Dorothea spoke up firmly. "No," she said, "it wouldn't."

Mrs. Broom untied Dorothea's sash and tied it again in a bow. "Why, Dorothea, I'm surprised."

"More cookies, anybody?" said Eleanor, heroically passing the plate. (It was hopeless. The tea party was a flop. She should have known. The whole thing was a big mistake. All that trouble, making the cookies and vacuuming the rug!) "Here, Georgie, have another cookie." Eleanor poked Georgie's watermelon shirt in a friendly way.

Aunt Alex had never been good at small talk. The only thing she wanted to say was "I'm sorry, Georgie." Instead she said, "Georgie dear, why don't you and Dorothea play outdoors for a little while?"

Georgie brightened, and looked at Dorothea. Dorothea hesitated, then slid slowly off her mother's lap.

"Put on your new coat, Dorothea," said Mrs. Broom, "and don't get it dirty, will you, dear?"

"What have you got to play with out here?" said Dorothea, staring around doubtfully on the front porch.

Georgie looked dumbly at Dorothea. What did she have to play with? Then she beamed. "Something wonderful! I'll show you!"

Something wonderful? Dorothea hurried eagerly after Georgie, almost stepping on Georgie's heels with her shiny shoes. But at the entrance to the bush house she paused and hung back while Georgie scrambled inside on all fours. Bending down with her hands on her chubby knees, Dorothea stared inside. "I don't think I want to go in there," she said.

Georgie was holding the branches aside. She watched with surprise as the top half of Dorothea disappeared. Now she could see only Dorothea's white socks and shiny shoes waiting stolidly at the door of the bush house.

For a moment longer Georgie kneeled within her house and looked out. Beyond Dorothea's legs she could see the Mill Brook meadow. There were swamp maples growing beside the brook, their small leaves red as fire. And below the ridge the long stumpy branches of the dying elm tree were in full majesty of leaf, arching their yellow chains far out over Lexington Road. Somewhere a cricket was rasping one leg against another. The sun was spattering through the forsythia boughs. It was lovely and private in Georgie's bush house. If only she could stay there! If only Dorothea would go back to her mother and leave her alone!

But Georgie knew she had to be a good sport. She had to try to give Dorothea a good time.

She crawled out of the bush house and stood up beside Dorothea. Little pieces of leaves clung to her puffy jacket. Her knees were dirty. There was a twig in her hair.

"Let's watch TV, okay?" said Dorothea, gazing at Georgie.

"Well, okay," said Georgie, not looking at Dorothea.

28

MISS PRAWN KEEPS HER EYES PEELED

ON THE LAST DAY OF the hunting season Miss Prawn rose at five A.M., just as usual. She was merely following her weekly schedule, which called for cleaning the living room at five o'clock every Saturday morning.

It was no small task, there were so many surfaces to rush at with the dustcloth—all the little tables and dressers and the gold jars and the knickknacks and the bric-a-brac. The antique hat pins must be removed from the pincushion one by one and dusted and polished and stuck back in. The doilies and dresser scarves had to be washed and starched. Of course it was impossible to clean the ostrich feathers, but at least they could be shaken out and combed. And every one of the pillows and bolsters and sofa cushions must be plumped and fluffed into a high marshmallowy mound. Last but not least there was the enormous fern in the window to be dabbed at with a wet dishrag, frond by frond.

It was while Miss Prawn was jabbing her dustcloth into the woven pattern of the wicker fern stand that a thought struck her. She put down her dustcloth, sank into the chair in front of her desk, opened her book of reveries, and wrote in a flowing hand across the top of a clean page,

This morning my thoughts hover like the fluttering wings of a butterfly.

Oh, wasn't that good! Miss Prawn read the passage over and smiled with justifiable pride. After all, it wasn't everyone in the town of Concord who was forwarding the cause of Art and Literature this early on a Saturday morning! She paused, waiting for a new burst of inspiration, poising her pen over the page, her gaze fixed dreamily out the window on the house next door.

And then, once again, Miss Prawn saw something that startled her, something that straightened her back with determination, giving direction to her life and meaning to her day. Clapping shut her book of reveries, she snatched up a piece of letter paper and began writing a note to her employer. She would seal it, mark it *PERSONAL*, and send it by special messenger (that chubby little Dorothea Broom across the street). Miss Prawn had become addicted to writing notes. It was much more exciting than telephoning.

Dear Ralph, [scribbled Miss Prawn]

I am sorry to say that I have beheld no further miraculous flights by the child in the house next door. She was ill for a while, I understand, and has only recently emerged from the sickroom. But I write now in haste to inform you that a Foreign Party is threatening her in some way. Something WITH WINGS is in the neighborhood. I catch glimpses of it from time to time, a SHAPE hovering in the sky at dusk, a wing flapping over the roof at the first glimmering of dawn. Considering its size, I would judge it to be either a small angel or a rather important and distinguished fairy.

Note: Tonight the moon will be full. I will keep a sharp eye out for trouble. I will stand true. You can rely on me.

Be strong! Be strong! We are not here to play!
Maltbie D. Babcock, 1901

171

Awake, my soul! stretch every nerve,
And press with vigour on. . . .

> *Phillip Doddridge, 1755*

Speak, and behold! we answer!
Command, and we obey!

> *John Haynes Holmes, 1913*

> (Keep your eyes peeled, Ralph)
> As ever,
> Madeline

29

TOO BIG FOR FLYING

*U*NCLE FREDDY WAS TRYING to clear the front yard of leaves before suppertime. The springy bamboo rake vibrated in his hands. The leaves flew before it into a pile. It was only six o'clock, but the sun had already set and red shreds of clouds were rushing across the western sky. It was cold. Uncle Freddy shivered in his thin coat. Then he noticed Miss Prawn in the yard next door, and he leaned across the sharp spears of her yucca plants to say hello. "Good heavens, Madeline," he said, "you're not digging up those flowers of yours? Well, I suppose you're only being sensible. It will be winter soon, and they *would* look out of place, blossoming in the middle of a snow bank."

Miss Prawn had been down on her knees. But now she sat up and looked at Uncle Freddy in surprise. "Digging them up? Oh, no, I'm not digging them up. I'm just grubbing out the weeds. That's why I chose plastic flowers in the first place. They never fade. In rain or snow, hail or sleet, they will still say WELCOME TO CONCORD, proclaiming our hospitality to the whole world! They will always look good as new."

"Or bad as new," muttered Uncle Freddy under his breath, turning away, climbing the porch stairs, abandoning the leaf-raking job for the day.

"Oh, Fred," called Miss Prawn, getting up to her full height, waving her weeding fork at him, "have you noticed the moon? Take a look at the moon. It's full again. Don't say I didn't warn you. Take care."

Uncle Freddy looked over his shoulder at the great pale orb of the full moon rising to the east over the meadow. "Yes, yes, of course. Thank you, Madeline. Thank you for your concern." Actually it irritated Uncle Freddy to have his nosy neighbor tell him how to take care of his own little stepdaughter. But he would never say so out loud. After all—one had to face up to it—Miss Prawn's warning had been correct before. Hideously, horribly, precisely correct.

Inside the house Aunt Alex was throwing supper together in the dark kitchen, setting the table, turning out the meat loaf on a platter.

"My dear, how can you see?" Uncle Freddy flicked the light switch, and the lamp dropped a cone of brilliance over the table. Instantly the dull china glistened with a blue stripe and the lettuce turned a vivid green and the meat loaf a succulent steaming brown. High over the hanging lamp the tops of the cupboards disappeared in the shadowy gloom of the high kitchen ceiling.

Aunt Alex poured milk, foaming white, into the glasses, and shook her head. "I hate turning on the light," she said. "It feels like winter, to turn the light on at suppertime. And tomorrow it will be worse. Tonight the time changes. The sun will set a whole hour earlier tomorrow. Oh, it's too bad. It's too soon."

"Well, at least we'll all get an extra hour of sleep," said Uncle Freddy brightly. "Think of it! A twenty-five-hour day, a whole hour tucked in before tomorrow begins, an hour plucked from eternity, an hour that doesn't exist, when anything could happen! The dead could arise! The stars and the moon might dance in their courses!"

Talk at suppertime was about Arthur Hathaway. Arthur was the school's worst student, the most hopeless, and the most charming at the same time. Uncle Freddy poked his fork in his salad and groaned. "The boy can talk a blue streak, that's what's so confusing. He can enchant the whole class, including me. But he doesn't read the assignments. He just thinks he does. Oh, yes, Arthur really thinks he's read everything, but he hasn't. Not one single thing."

Eleanor turned her empty milk glass around and around. "You'll have to admit, though, he's really good-looking," she said, glancing up at Aunt Alex.

"Good-looking?" said Aunt Alex. "Arthur Hathaway? Well, yes, I suppose he is good-looking." Aunt Alex got up from the table and went to the stove. "Oh, that Arthur Hathaway!" Hanging over the coffeepot with her face flushed, damp hair clinging to her forehead, Aunt Alex didn't notice Georgie slipping out of the kitchen into the hall in a stream of cats.

Only Eleanor looked up and called after her, "Give Dollabella a big kiss for me, okay, Georgie?"

In the hall Georgie found Eddy coming down the stairs. "Hey, Georgie," said Eddy, "don't you want to see my moon rocket glow in the dark? Look, it's all finished."

"Oh, wow, Eddy," said Georgie, "that's really great." But when Eddy went into the kitchen, Georgie lingered in the hall, gazing up at the twelve stairs to the second floor.

In the kitchen Eddy stood dramatically in the doorway. "Behold!" he said, switching off the light. In the sudden darkness his moon rocket floated, a ghostly green specter, a phosphorescent vision. Eddy spun slowly in one place and the rocket swept eerily over his head in a glowing circle.

"Hey, that's pretty good," said Eleanor.

"Well, now, Eddy, that's really beautiful," said Aunt Alex.

"Why, Eddy," began Uncle Freddy—

And then there was a noise, a thumping in the hall, and a sharp cry.

"Oh, no!" Eleanor jumped to her feet. "Not again! Not Georgie again!" Charging at the door, she collided with Aunt Alex.

"Oh, Georgie *dear*," cried Aunt Alex.

The four of them tumbled out into the hall and rushed to pick up Georgie. They found her whimpering on the floor at the foot of the stairs.

"Darling *child*," said Uncle Freddy, "are you all right?"

Georgie looked at him, her face screwed up in tears.

"There now," said Aunt Alex. Picking up Georgie, she sat down on the stairs.

Georgie sat up stiffly in Aunt Alex's arms, her legs sprawling. "I'm all right," she said. "I won't try it anymore. I'm too big now, I guess. I'm just too big for flying."

Over Georgie's head Uncle Freddy and Aunt Alex and Eleanor and Eddy exchanged glances of relief. But beside them in the curve of the stairs Henry Thoreau gazed with his marble eyes more solemnly than ever in the direction of Walden Pond. His stony brow was wrinkled with foreboding.

30

A FAIR EXCHANGE

*T*HE GOOSE PRINCE pulled himself out of the water and dragged himself up on the shore of Walden Pond. He was worn out. His shoulder muscles ached and he was lame. One of the lead pellets from the shotgun blast that had wounded the child had spent itself deep in the fleshy muscle of his left leg. It was still there, imbedded, festering, giving him pain at every step. Savagely now he pecked at a parasite at the base of his tail, and then, slowly, he began to limp up the steep hill, half lurching on his webbed feet, half flapping upward with his wings. At last he waddled drunkenly into the clearing. He had come for the present.

He must see the little girl again. To say good-bye and

give her the present. But how? The Goose Prince hooted softly with worry. The man with the gun was everywhere, and the child was nowhere! Oh, he had seen her once or twice out-of-doors, and he had rejoiced to observe that she was all right. But she was never alone. Twice he had come floundering down on the porch roof and pecked at the glass, but she had not come to the window. He had peered inside, but he had seen nothing. The room was empty. Perhaps the little girl was afraid.

Sorrowfully, the Goose Prince told himself that the child had a right to be afraid.

But how was he to give her the present?

Painfully he limped across the clearing, hobbling to spare his throbbing leg, and paused beside one of the granite posts. Lowering his dizzy head to the place where he had buried the present in a cover of leaves, the Goose Prince shuffled with his webbed feet until he found it. The present lay shining in a nest of wizened grass and maple seeds and goldenrod and crumpled bouquets of asters and a clutter of pebbles and acorn caps—gifts from the child.

It was only an exchange he wanted to make, a fair exchange. One present in exchange for the others.

Gently the Goose Prince picked up Georgie's present and carried it away in his beak.

31

THE CLEVERNESS OF GEORGIE

*S*HE WAS TOO BIG for flying. Georgie knew that.

So she would only say good-bye.

Tonight at midnight it would at last be safe to say good-bye. The hunting season would be over at midnight.

The Goose Prince was not far away. Georgie had caught excited glimpses of him. He was hiding somewhere nearby, hiding and waiting. But now the waiting was nearly over. How could she call to him secretly, silently, at midnight?

Georgie was clever. She had figured out a way.

Now she lay in bed, her head next to Dollabella on the pillow. Eleanor's alarm clock was a lump under the

181

covers. Every now and then Georgie put her head under the covers and looked at the clock. The numbers on the face of the clock glowed in the dark, green like Eddy's moon rocket. The hands moved slowly. Slowly, slowly the minutes turned into quarter hours, and the quarter hours into half hours, and the half hours into hours. Georgie knew the time would pass more quickly if she went to sleep, but she didn't dare. What if she didn't wake up again till morning? Of course she could set the alarm clock to wake her up at midnight, but then Eleanor would wake up at midnight too. And that would never do.

So she must keep watch, and look at the clock.

It was ten-twenty-two . . .

Ten-forty-seven . . .

Eleven-thirteen . . .

Eleven-thirty-seven . . .

The minute hand was creeping closer and closer to the top of the clock. . . .

There was only a little crack between the minute hand and the hour hand. . . .

Now the crack was gone. The two hands were pointing straight up. It was exactly midnight.

But still Georgie huddled in her bed. Relentlessly she forced herself to wait another five minutes. . . .

Then five minutes more. Because the clock might be

fast. You couldn't be sure. And she must be absolutely certain that the last day of the hunting season had come and gone, that it had vanished into yesterday forever.

So it was fifteen minutes after twelve o'clock midnight by Eleanor's alarm clock when Georgie slipped out of bed and pulled on her bathrobe. The bathrobe was too short for her now, and the sleeves felt tight under the arms. Her slippers were too short too. She had to curl her toes to keep them on.

The doorknob mustn't click. Georgie turned the knob slowly until it unlatched, and then she turned it back the other way just as slowly. There. Gently she drew the door inward and padded out into the hall, feeling the large empty darkness expand around her. Softly she crept downstairs. The moon was shining behind the house somewhere, but not a sliver of moonlight shone into the front hall. Georgie had to feel her way, clinging to the stair railing, sliding her hand around the polished skirts of the metal woman on the newel post, trailing her fingers across the marble nose of Henry Thoreau. But moonlight was pouring through the windows of the kitchen, and when she stepped softly down the back steps, it was flooding the whole outdoors.

The rest was easy. The wet grass made no noise under Georgie's slippered feet. Boldly she walked right through the laundry hanging on the line, smelling the sunshine trapped in her mother's blouse as it slipped over her face. But the yucca hedge was a problem. Its multitudinous sharp points bristled at Georgie in the moonlight. Backing up, she clenched her fists, then ran forward and *jumped*—whee! a tremendous jump—and *thump!* she was down on the other side. Breathing hard, Georgie looked back at the yucca hedge. It had been an ordinary jump. There had been no floating, no lifting and drifting down to the ground—just her new long legs carrying her safely up and over. (Oh well, thought Georgie, at least long legs are good for something.)

In the dim yard of the neighboring house, Miss Prawn's artificial garden was brightly visible. The plastic roses glowed weirdly in the dark—like Eddy's moon rocket, like the phosphorescent numbers on Eleanor's alarm clock—bidding a vulgar

WELCOME TO CONCORD

to any belated tourist who might be sauntering down Walden Street in the middle of the night.

Folding her arms on her chest, Georgie looked at the flower bed. Then she walked firmly to one end of it, reached out her hand, grasped one of the plastic roses, and *jerked* it out of the ground. She jerked out another. Georgie jerked and jerked, plucking one flower at a time, piling the stiff sprays beside her on the ground.

After a while she moved to the other side of the garden and began pulling out more flowers. But then she thought of Miss Prawn. As the new pile of uprooted roses grew bigger, she couldn't help glancing up furtively at the second-story windows of Miss Prawn's house. High and gray and square, the house loomed above the garden. But the windows were empty. There was no horrified face looking down at Georgie, screeching *STOP, STOP.* (Georgie didn't know it, but the indomitable Miss Prawn had abandoned her commitment to watch and wait. She was sleeping at her post. She had failed to *awake her soul! stretch every nerve, And press with vigour on.* She was not standing *firm to the fight.* She was disobedient *behold! to her own command.* But it wasn't her fault. Poor Madeline had risen as usual that morning at the crack of dawn, and by eleven P.M. she simply couldn't keep her eyes peeled a moment longer. She had gone yawning up to bed. She was sleeping the sleep of the just.)

So Georgie went right on pulling the roses out of Miss Prawn's flower bed until only four letters were left out of the sixteen that had so recently proclaimed their *WELCOME TO CONCORD.*

The remaining four letters still spelled a word, a perfectly good word.

COME

said the flowers.

Georgie stood back and looked with satisfaction at the new flowery message in Miss Prawn's garden. Then she picked up all the roses that were lying on the ground, stuffed them under a sprawling bush, leaped back over the sharp dagger points of the barrier between the two houses, and hurried around the side of her own house to the front porch steps.

Solemnly she climbed them—one, two, three—and then she sat down on the top step to wait.

COME

said the flowers in Miss Prawn's garden.

COME
COME
COME

32

ANOTHER CHANCE
FOR MR. PREEK

M<small>R. PREEK'S CAR WAS</small> parked across Walden Street beside the Mill Brook meadow. He had been drowsing over the wheel, but now he jerked himself awake and looked at his watch. In glowing red numbers it said

12:28:31.

That meant it was twenty-eight minutes and thirty-one seconds after midnight.

12:28:32 . . .

12:28:33 . . .

Ralph Preek pulled himself upright. Feeling for the button on the side of his watch, he pressed it with his forefinger. Instantly the number 12 changed back to the number 11. The time was now

11:28:58 . . .

11:28:59 . . .

11:29:00

precisely.

Mr. Preek smiled gloomily at his digital watch in the warm shadowy privacy of his car. With a flick of his finger he had extended the hunting season. Along with every other human being up and down the entire length of the eastern seaboard he had been given another hour to live over again.

And then he had slept through half of it.

Well, what did it matter, anyway? His cause was hopeless. The bird had been too wily for him. Oh, it was still around somewhere, he was sure of that. He had caught sight of it just the other day at Walden Pond. It had been flying low over the trees with something in its beak, and he had fired a wild, crazy shot, but he had missed. He had thought it was his last chance. But then

Madeline had written him a letter. She had said something was hanging around the neighboring house. It was an angel, Madeline said. Or a fairy! Well, that was Madeline for you. As a personal secretary the woman was efficiency itself, but in every other way she was as nutty as a fruitcake. The thing wasn't an angel or a fairy. It was the colossal bird he had seen so many times before. And its fiendish purpose was clearer than ever. It was still trying to kidnap the little girl and carry her away to its gruesome nest on some rocky mountaintop, where it would tear at her vitals and crush her fragile bones in its terrible beak. (Mr. Preek was remembering a television show he had once seen about the habits of bald eagles.)

Of course he had reacted at once to Madeline's letter. He had spent the entire day lurking in the neighborhood, keeping an eye on the house, looking for the dangerous creature to show itself. But to no avail. The hunting season was over, and he had failed.

But, no, it wasn't over, not quite yet. Ralph Preek felt for his gun on the seat beside him. The polished wood and oiled steel felt comfortable under his hand. It had taken a lot of careful labor to get the thing back in A1 condition, after he had retrieved it from that swamp at Walden Pond. But he had spared no effort. There was no speck of rust on the barrel. The mechanism was working perfectly. And now there was still another half hour left, thirty minutes more of deadly opportunity. He would make one more foray around the house on foot, just to see what he could see.

Cautiously Mr. Preek opened the door of his car and heaved himself out of the front seat. Softly he walked to the other side of the street and peered through the hedge into the front yard of the tall house with its broad porch and moon-washed tower. Then he gasped.

The bird was standing on the walk.

The girl was sitting on the front porch. She was staring at the bird. She was mesmerized. . . .

33

FAREWELL

*T*HE GOOSE PRINCE had appeared from nowhere. One moment he wasn't there, the next moment he was. He was standing stock-still on one foot, his pale breast gleaming. Something lay on the walk in front of him. Something small and round.

Georgie stood up, feeling a smile spread all over her face. She began walking down the porch steps. Then she stopped short, startled, because the Goose Prince had jerked his head back. He was hooting with surprise.

It was because she had grown so tall! Georgie looked down at herself, smiling ruefully at the length of bare white legs gangling below her bathrobe, and whispered, "I'm sorry I got so big."

"It's all right," said the Goose Prince. Then Georgie saw the small bumps beside his beak that meant he was smiling too. "My, my, just look at you. Well, isn't that nice."

"Thank you for coming," whispered Georgie. "I just wanted to say good-bye."

The Goose Prince shifted his weight, wincing dizzily at the ache in his left leg, and then he lowered his head and poked at the thing that lay on the walk in front of him. It rolled a little to one side and came to rest in Uncle Freddy's pile of leaves. "I brought you the present," he said.

"The present?" said Georgie. She had forgotten about the present. "Oh, thank you." She ran down the last step and bent down to the Goose Prince and hugged him, nestling her head in the old place between the beginning of his long neck and the base of his wing. "Good-bye," whispered Georgie. "Will you come back next year?"

"Next year?" Gently the Goose Prince brushed Georgie's sleeve with his wing. "Next year! Well! I'll try. Well, yes, certainly. Next year! I will certainly try." Then he stood back in all his princely dignity and inclined his head. "The present—take good care of it."

Georgie nodded. She couldn't speak. Lifting one hand, she watched the Goose Prince turn away from her and make a limping rush at the night air. Why was he running all to one side? Had he forgotten how to fly? Georgie looked on in dismay as the Goose Prince blundered across the grass, flapping and heaving in a frantic effort to lift his heavy body from the ground. At last he was airborne, and now he was circling over her, looking down. Georgie lifted her face and her two hands in farewell. . . .

The bird was an easy target. Ralph Preek sighted along the barrel and pulled the trigger lightly. There was a deafening report. The bird dropped at the feet of the little girl.

For an instant Mr. Preek thought to his horror that he had wounded the child as well, because she made a tremendous leap into the air. But then he could see that she was all right. She was standing still, staring at the dead bird. Now she was throwing herself down on the tumbled heap of feathers.

Ralph Preek lowered his gun and smiled with grim satisfaction. He walked across the street, got back in his car, and drove away, as the bell in the steeple of the First Parish Church began ringing midnight for the second time.

34

THE PRESENT DISAPPEARS

UNCLE FREDDY BURIED the Goose Prince the next morning at Walden Pond. He didn't ask anyone's permission. He just did it.

Georgie chose the place. Walking stiffly from the car, she led Uncle Freddy to the clearing where the granite posts stood upright around the old house site, and then she stopped and said, "Here."

The place seemed right to Uncle Freddy. It had been his own private opinion that the Goose Prince was Henry Thoreau come back to life, reincarnated, back in the world as a noble bird! So it seemed altogether proper to bury him at the place where Henry had lived at Walden Pond.

* * *

The present had disappeared. Georgie looked for it everywhere. She was frantic. Over and over again she remembered the last words of the Goose Prince—*Take good care of it.* And yet she had lost it! She must find it, she *must*!

"Oh, poor Georgie, what *is* she doing?" Aunt Alex watched through the window as Georgie picked up handfuls of leaves and scrabbled frantically with her fingers in the grass and tossed more leaves from one side of the walk to the other.

"She must be looking for something," said Eddy, and he went outdoors to help.

But Georgie couldn't explain what she was looking for.

"A present?" said Eddy. "Well, what kind of present was it? What did it look like?"

"I think it was round," said Georgie. Her face was pinched. She poked along the fence among the drooping flowers. "It was little, I think, and round. Sort of round."

But the present from the Goose Prince was nowhere to be found. Eddy and Georgie looked for it all over the front yard and the backyard. They looked for it in the street and in the grass on the other side of the road. They looked beneath the porch and under hedges and behind bushes, until the first snowflakes of the season began to fall, and then Eddy persuaded Georgie to come inside.

It was only a light flurry. For an hour or two the snow lay thinly on the ground, with brown leaves and green blades of grass pricking up through it, and then the afternoon sun melted it away. But Georgie didn't go outdoors again to look for the present. She had given up.

Uncle Freddy was in the kitchen when the terrible scraping and thumping began over his head. Running upstairs, he found Georgie trying desperately to wedge the head of her bed through the door of Eleanor's room.

"Dear *child*," said Uncle Freddy, "let me help you. You have to take the bed apart." Heaving at the mattress, he unhooked the pieces of Georgie's bed and carried them across the hall and set them up again in her old room. Aunt Alex made the bed up nicely, with clean sheets and pillowcases and fresh blankets and good old Dollabella, while Uncle Freddy stalked over to Georgie's window and yanked out the nails with the claw of his hammer.

And then Georgie climbed into her bed and pulled up the covers and lay down flat on her back as if she would never get up again.

On Monday morning she didn't come downstairs. Aunt Alex brought Georgie her breakfast in bed. She didn't make her go to school. Nor did she ask Georgie to get up the next day—or the next. Day after day Georgie lay in bed silently, her arms rigid at her sides, staring at the ceiling. Aunt Alex sat quietly nearby, sewing or correcting papers. Georgie didn't talk. She didn't read. She ate almost nothing. And she didn't cry. That is, she didn't cry in the daytime.

But she cried at night. Across the hall Eleanor would hear small strangled sobs and the murmur of Aunt Alex's voice or tender noises from Uncle Freddy. After a while the sobbing would stop, and Aunt Alex or Uncle Freddy would stumble back to bed, and in the morning they would be hollow-eyed and anxious and pale. And in the morning Georgie would stay home from school again and spend another day in bed.

She stayed in bed for a week. But on Monday morning of the second week Georgie got out of bed and came down to breakfast. Standing in the doorway of the kitchen, she announced solemnly, "I'm all right now."

"Well, Georgie!" Uncle Freddy jumped out of his chair and patted her arm and fixed her a big bowl of cereal and poured too much milk into the bowl. The milk washed over the brim onto the table.

"Oh, you're so clumsy, Uncle Freddy!" Eleanor rushed happily for the sponge to clean up the table.

"Wow," shouted Eddy, "it's all over the floor." Dropping to his knees, he mopped it up with a paper napkin.

"Would you like some fruit on your cereal, Georgie dear?" Aunt Alex snatched up a banana from the sideboard.

They were all trying hard. Georgie was trying hardest of all. She said thank you and swallowed her breakfast and tried to smile.

And then at last she went to school. And at school she opened her notebook and copied her spelling paper and did her arithmetic neatly and came home with her papers marked *100* and *GOOD* and *A*, just as usual.

And after school there was a lot of cheery talk and things to do, all calculated to help Georgie feel like herself again. From the parlor came the buzzing whine of the sewing machine, where Eleanor was making Georgie a new dress. From the cellar rose the noisy banging of hammers, where Uncle Freddy and Eddy were building a bookcase for Georgie's room. From the kitchen drifted the soft murmur of Aunt Alex's voice, reading aloud to Georgie. Everyone was trying to bolster Georgie's courage. What if it faltered? What if she went back to bed and didn't get up in the morning?

But she did. On Tuesday morning Georgie went off to school just as usual, just as if nothing had ever happened. Everything seemed to be back to normal.

Eleanor knew it was a shaky normalcy. Georgie was putting on a good show, but you could tell she was still miserable inside. The poor little kid, she always took things so hard. She *felt* things so. She was quiet, that was the reason. Still waters ran deep, that was what everybody said. And that was Georgie for you.

On Tuesday afternoon Eleanor came home from school with Georgie heavily on her mind. Opening the front door, stepping into the hall, she called, "Georgie? Georgie, where are you?"

The house was warm. Coming in from the cold Eleanor was immediately engulfed by the dark comfort of the front hall. Her nose quivered. The furnace had been turned on, and every day the hot air from the radiators sank deeper into the spongy interiors of the sofas and chairs. And now there was a fragrance of coats and sweaters shaken out of windowseats, of blankets unfolded and tossed out, ballooning, over beds. Eleanor pulled off her coat, suddenly remembering the time last March when she had stayed at home with a cold, when she had lain comfortably on the sofa in the parlor with three pillows under her head and a heavy down puff on her knees and mugs of cocoa and plates of cinnamon toast on the table beside her. The mixed perfume of heavy sweaters and woolen blankets and boiling radiators brought it all back to Eleanor, the comfortable feeling of the house in the wintertime.

Where was Georgie? The kitchen door burst open.

Aunt Alex's students were pouring out into the hall, carrying stacks of cups and saucers, heading for an afternoon class in the parlor. They were laughing and talking and clashing crockery down on the parlor table.

"Well, if it isn't young Eleanor," said Arthur Hathaway gallantly. "*Hello there*, Eleanor." Arthur was carrying the heavy coffee urn. He stared after Eleanor as she hurried past him into the kitchen to look for Georgie.

Eleanor could feel the back of her head being looked at. Ordinarily it would have felt nice, being looked at by Arthur Hathaway. But today all she could think about was Georgie.

Aunt Alex was pouring milk into a pitcher, putting the pitcher on a tray with a bowl of sugar. She glanced up quickly at Eleanor. "She's upstairs," said Aunt Alex. "In her room."

"In her room?" said Eleanor. "Oh, no, she hasn't gone to bed again?"

"I don't think so. She's all right. See if you can find something for her to do."

Eleanor ran upstairs, calling brightly for Georgie. She knocked on Georgie's bedroom door. "Georgie, are you in there? May I come in?"

There was a pause, then the creaky spring of Georgie's bed. Then Georgie opened her door and smiled bravely at Eleanor.

"Well, Georgie!" Eleanor breezed into Georgie's room and darted a glance at the bed. It was a little rumpled, as if someone had been lying on top of the spread. The window was open. "Oh, brrrr," said Eleanor, shivering. She went to the window and closed it smartly, with a *bang*. "Well, now, Georgie, what would you like to do this afternoon?"

Georgie looked out the window. A flurry of small birds darted across her view and disappeared. She tried to think. "Shall we play outdoors?"

"Outdoors?" said Eleanor. "Oh, well, okay. I mean, it's cold out there, but never mind. Do you want to wear my turquoise sweater?"

Georgie nodded and smiled. Eleanor brought the sweater from her dresser across the hall and pulled it down over Georgie's head. "What shall we do outdoors?" said Eleanor.

Georgie's head poked through the sweater. "Shall we have another tea party?" she said.

"Well, why not?" said Eleanor valiantly. (Oh, brrrr, a tea party out-of-doors in November. Well, anything to please Georgie.)

No longer did the bush house feel like a secret place. The leaves that had covered it like a spreading parasol had fallen to the ground, and now the bare branches of forsythia dropped cold bolts of wintry sunshine on the tea party within.

Eleanor and Georgie settled themselves luxuriously on comfortable cushions of drifted leaves. "Oh, look, Georgie," said Eleanor, "there's an acorn. And there's another one. They've just fallen from the oak trees. We can make Dollabella a whole new set of dishes."

"Oh, good," said Georgie, and together they began poking in the leaves, looking for more.

But it was Georgie who found something better than acorns.

"Why, Georgie," said Eleanor, "where did that come from? It looks brand-new."

"It is," said Georgie. Joyfully she held it up in both hands. "It's the present. It's the one I was looking for."

35

THE PRESENT AT LAST

*I*T WAS A RUBBER BALL. A small rubber ball with blue and white streaks. After the shotgun blast that had killed the Goose Prince, during the tumult and confusion and despair and the rush of people all over the front yard, the ball had been kicked into the bush house. It had buried itself in the drifted leaves.

"The present?" said Eleanor. "Well, well, so that's what the present is." Privately Eleanor didn't think a small rubber ball was much of a present, but she didn't say so. Georgie seemed to be happy with it. "Why don't we play catch in the driveway?"

"All right," said Georgie eagerly. Together they rustled out of the bush house on hands and knees, and then

203

they stood up in the gravel driveway and tossed the ball back and forth between them.

It was a good ball for throwing, hard and firm enough to fly straight and true, making perfect, easy flights, and light enough to drop gently into the waiting hand. "Oh, good catch, Georgie," said Eleanor.

Eddy too was a little disappointed in the present. Georgie showed it to him in the kitchen at suppertime. "So that's it," he said, and then he tossed it playfully at the ceiling once or twice. "It's a pretty good ball, I guess. Here, Georgie, catch."

Georgie caught the ball in both hands and giggled at Eddy. Uncle Freddy nudged Aunt Alex, and Aunt Alex caught Eleanor's eye. Georgie's smile was real and broad and proud. The discovery of the missing present seemed to be all that was needed to bring her back to herself altogether. And if it would do that for Georgie, it was a very fine present indeed.

But it was Georgie herself who discovered the best thing about the present from the Goose Prince.

She had just said good night, and Aunt Alex and Uncle Freddy had looked up from the papers they were grading and Eddy had looked up from the TV and Eleanor had looked up from her homework, and they had all said, "Good night, Georgie." She had walked to the stairs and put her foot on the bottom step. And then she had held up her rubber ball to show it to Henry Thoreau, standing so quietly on his marble stand in the curve of the stairs.

"Look," Georgie whispered, "it's the present. I found it. It was safe in the leaves out there in the yard all the time. I didn't lose it after all."

Dreamily Henry gazed at the ball in Georgie's hand. And then to her surprise, something strange began to happen.

In the half-dark of the front hall the ball was glowing dimly. Georgie was reminded of the way Eddy's plastic rocket ship had glimmered in the dark. Instead of climbing the stairs, she opened the door of the coat closet, pushed through the heavy coats, and pulled the door shut behind her. Then in the absolute blackness at the back of the coat closet, she held up the ball that was her present from the Goose Prince and looked at it.

It was glowing brightly in the dark! It was! Like the moon rocket! But with a radiance very different from the weird green phosphorescence of Eddy's rocket ship. The streaks on the surface of the glowing blue ball were luminous with a pure white light.

And then Georgie gasped. The ball was lifting from her fingers, rising into the air. It was poising lightly above her hand. It was growing larger. The close, muffled space in the back of the coat closet was opening out. The walls and the coats were falling away, becoming a vast darkness, empty but for Georgie and the great gleaming ball that hung before her, turning slowly and majestically in the immense and impalpable night. The blue surface of the ball was streaked with clouds, and below the clouds Georgie could catch glimpses of great land masses, of dark continents and snow-covered ice caps and deep jungles and blue oceans and lofty mountain ranges—the Andes, the Alps, the Himalayas.

"Oh," breathed Georgie. "It's the world. It's the whole world."

It was true. The gift from the Goose Prince was an image of the earth itself, shining and turning in the stupendous immensity of the coat closet under the stairs in the front hall of the big house at No. 40 Walden Street in Concord, Massachusetts.

Take good care of it, the Goose Prince had said.

"Oh, yes," whispered Georgie, renewing her promise with all her heart. "I will. Oh, yes, I will."

Slowly the ball stopped turning and began to grow smaller once again. In a moment it looked like an ordinary rubber ball. It was hardly glowing at all. Georgie held her hand under it, and the ball dropped lightly into her palm. She took it upstairs, showed it proudly to Dollabella, tucked it safely under her pillow, hopped into bed, put her head down on the pillow, and went to sleep.

And nothing woke her until morning, not even the racket in the sky just after she fell asleep, as a last tardy flock of wild geese flew over the house, cleaving the air in a battering plunge, heading for Walden Pond, eager to break the fragile ice with the fury of their clamorous descent. Low over the peaked roof and domed tower of Georgie's house they were shouting at each other, *Go DOWN! go DOWN! follow ME! follow WHERE? right THERE? over THERE? no, HERE! come HERE! come HERE! HERE! HERE! right HERE! come DOWN! right HERE!*